LIVE WIRE

CRISTIN HARBER

BOOKS BY CRISTIN HARBER

THE TITAN SERIES:
Book 1: Winters Heat (Colby Winters)

Book 1.5: Sweet Girl (Prequel to Garrison's Creed)

Book 2: Garrison's Creed (Cash Garrison)

Book 3: Westin's Chase (Jared Westin)

Book 4: Gambled (Brock Gamble)

Book 5: Chased (Asher McIntyre)

Book 6: Savage Secrets (Rocco Savage)

Book 7: Hart Attack (Roman Hart)

Book 8: Black Dawn (Parker Black)

Book 8.5: Live Wire (Jared & Sugar Westin)

Book 9: Bishop's Queen (Bishop O'Kane)

Book 10: Locke and Key (Locke Oliver)

THE DELTA SERIES:
Book 1: Delta: Retribution

Book 2: Delta: Revenge

Book 3: Delta: Rescue

Delta novella in Liliana Hart's MacKenzie Family Collection

THE ONLY SERIES:
Book 1: Only for Him
Book 2: Only for Her
Book 3: Only for Us
Book 4: Only Forever

Each Titan and Delta book can be read as a standalone (except for Sweet Girl), but readers will likely best enjoy the series in order. The Only series must be read in order.

LIVE WIRE

PROLOGUE

Thirty Years Ago

"WAKE UP!"

Jared Westin's eyes flew open as he took in the unfamiliar room of his grandparents' house. The smoke was faint enough that he wouldn't have noticed it if he hadn't heard his dad's strict voice order him awake.

The door flew open. "Get up. Jared. William. Wake up. Get downstairs. Get outside."

Dad was nothing if not a man of few words. Each had purpose and value. So many slung together meant that Jared had to snap to and do as he was told. But he yawned—confused and tired—and rubbed his sleepy eyes. He didn't want to get out of bed.

His mom rushed into the room. "Let's go. Hurry."

The heavy waft of burned plastic followed Mom as

1

she stood in her robe. The scent wasn't like candles a Christmas services. It was destructive and made hi nose wrinkle. Jared knew by his mom's tone that thi was more than his by-the-book parents doing what they did best: drilling rules and playing it safe. "William There's a fire. Wake up." He threw a pillow at hi cousin with high-school-level precision. "Fire. William Wake up."

"Huh?" William stirred and sat upright, groggily mopping his face with the back of his hand. "Fire?"

Jared grabbed William's wrist, dragging him from the other twin bed. "Come on, get up." Jared couldn' see fire or smoke, and nothing was warm. The only warning came from panicked parents and the stink, as i maybe Grandma had smoked too many of her cigarettes and set an ashtray on fire.

"But my mom and dad," William muttered. "I have to find."

"My dad will get them." Dad could do anything and get everybody to safety. He was a fireman now that he wasn't in the army anymore.

Jared heard a pop, and he and William jumped Then a door slammed. Someone yelled. There were a lot of people in this big, old house. Chaos had started. Doors opened and closed, some of them upstairs, others downstairs. Some of the older girls had set up a slumber party and slept on couches and in sleeping bags by the Christmas tree while his aunts and uncles had claimed bedrooms. He and William had won a game and gotten the room with the twin beds. But now they had to get outside.

"Wait," William cried, pulling against Jared's ten-year-old grip. "What about—"

"Come on." When there was a direction to follow. Simple. That was what to do in an emergency. Hadn't Uncle Matt taught him that? Dad would skin his hide if he didn't start moving boots fast. "We have to go."

"No." William's face froze in a panicked daze.

"Dang it, Will. This is what we do in emergencies. I'm older. Trust me already." No time to be scared. They could do that later—or William could. Jared wouldn't be scared of anything. He puffed out his chest and grabbed on to Will harder, but the air made his throat hurt.

The grown-up voices yelled. The noises came faster and scarier. His heart pounded. Sweat tickled his temples and neck at the collar, and he didn't know what to make of the commotion other than what he and William had been told to do: get out.

"Now!" And pulling William with everything he had, Jared dragged his concrete block of a cousin into the hall. Only then did William's legs start moving. What felt like minutes had only been seconds, and they moved downstairs.

"What's going on?" his cousin Kate asked as she hurried down the stairs with them.

Marlee bumped past them. "Fire!"

"There's no fire," Annie said from behind them "Jared, your dad is an overreacting buffoon."

He spun around and marched up to her. She'd been in trouble for sneaking out and coming back stoned every night they'd been at their grandparents'. "You don't know what you're talking about."

"Forget her." Marlee tugged him then grabbed William as they moved down the long staircase. "It's smoky."

Uncle Matt scooped Marlee up as he bounded in behind them. "Move it, kids."

Aunt Margarie took Jared's hand, and he looked over his shoulder to see Annie plodding behind. Their family swooshed out the door, hollering at Annie to follow close.

"I am!" she snapped.

As soon as they were outside, Aunt Margarie let go of him and lit into Annie. His cousin was right. Jared couldn't see fire—not even smoke. But the air tasted like burned dinner, only worse. It had coated his tongue, and his eyes were stinging. He looked for flames.

Wait. His heart dropped. His dog—where was Bucko? "Bucko!"

Aunt Margarie put a hand on his shoulder. "Hang on—"

Nope. There was no hanging on. Jared ran around

he crowd of family that had formed, searching for his
dog. "Anyone have Bucko?"

No answer.

"Hey." He stopped Kate. "Did you see Bucko?"

"Nope."

He approached the cousins who'd been downstairs
by the Christmas tree. "Did you guys get my dog?"

All heads shook.

Jared's throat tightened, and his eyes widened as he
turned back for the house. "Dad?" His parents wouldn't
forget Bucko. "Dad!"

There was no dog, and he didn't see Grandma,
Grandpa, Aunt Jilly, Uncle Brian, Mom, or Dad. The
neighbors milled in their yard, and he could see each
face—and the lack of his dog—under the illumination
of outdoor Christmas lights. "Where's Bucko?"

No one listened or turned. Frustration bubbled, and
his fists bunched uselessly. "Did anyone let my dog out
of his cage?"

Grandma had made him sleep in there. She said
something about how Bucko wanted to eat her
cigarettes, which wasn't true.

He looked at the imposing house. Black wood
shutters on an impressive white building. All was dark—
no Christmas lights shining on the outside of the house
anymore. It was the only one on the block without lights,
and now there was the bright, angry red light of a fire on
the opposite side to where Bucko was trapped.

5

Not on my watch. He was getting his dog. Jare
bolted toward the front door.

"Jared!"

"Get back over here!"

"Jared!"

The desperate yells for him didn't stop his bare fee
from running toward Bucko. He pushed through the
open door and heard the rumbling shouts of adult
arguing up the front staircase.

"Get out of the house, Jillian!" Uncle Brian shouted

"Christ. You too, Violet. Get out of this house."

That was his dad. Why Uncle Brian and Dad fough
with Mom and Aunt Jilly didn't matter—a huge
cracking noise sounded, and two screams let out.

"For God's sake. Brian, get them out," Dad yelled.

Jared crouched against the wall, watching Uncle
Brian carrying Aunt Jilly over his shoulder on the way
down the stairs and dragging his mom by the hand.

"Help my mom," Aunt Jillian cried.

No one noticed Jared, and that gave him a smidge
of relief because if Dad yelled at Mom like that—and
that *never* happened—then he must be really mad abou
people staying in the house, and he'd whip Jared'
bottom if he saw him there.

What felt like fifteen minutes since he'd run back
inside had probably only been seconds. The now heavy
smoke filled the house.

Bucko. Jared ran back to the back of the house. His

og was in the cage, whimpering and spinning in ircles. Jared pulled on the latch, and it wouldn't give. How did it unhook?

Jared could hear the consuming destruction of the ire, the noise of the house eating itself. He pulled on he metal latch, and it still wouldn't open. "Shoot."

Bucko barked, growled, jumped, and whined.

"I'm trying." Jared grabbed the cage and dragged it oward the door, but it wouldn't fit through the frame. "Dang it."

He coughed. His eyes watered. What was the rick? Bucko howled and cried. Jared thought about loing the same thing, but his dad wouldn't do something like that. Firemen didn't cry when the smoke became worse; military men didn't show lefeat. Dad would never back down, never leave his nan behind. "I'm trying, Bucko."

"Jared!"

He spun around, so lost in saving Bucko he hadn't heard anything other than his dog's cries.

"Violet! I found him," Jared's dad called, but his mom was nowhere to be seen. With a swift switch of he handle, he released Bucko, and the dog scampered oward the front of the house, nails scraping the floor. "C'mere, son. That's right. Never leave your man behind."

Jared nodded. Bucko was his man. His best riend. His dad was proud. That was how Dad had raised him. That was what Dad said over and over, and Jared had done the right thing. He beamed even as he coughed.

Dad scooped him up and ran the same path that Bucko had gone. With every footstep, he shouted, "Violet!"

They burst through the open front door, and fresh air hit his face. Jared gasped in clean breaths. Dad dropped him, and Bucko clobbered him.

"Where's Violet?" Dad shouted, pivoting, a man on a mission to find Mom.

"She hasn't come out yet," Uncle Brian said.

Aunt Jilly wrapped her arms around Jared. "Oh, baby. What did you do?"

"I had to get Bucko." Jared blinked, taking in the panic on her face. He spun for the house, pushing out of Aunt Jilly's arms. "Dad? Mom's still inside?"

The fire trucks finally arrived. Uncle Mark directed them to Grandma and Grandpa's room. Someone said, "That's John Westin's family's house. Do the best you can."

"I'm coming, Violet!" Dad charged back inside, and Jared flung himself to follow, Aunt Jilly catching him around the waist. The side of the house where his grandparents slept caved in as a burst of flames jumped—everyone hovering on the lawn gasped.

Aunt Jilly sobbed, pressing kisses to the top of his head. "How is this happening?"

He struggled out of her hold and turned to her, glaring because she would dare give up on his parents. "They're coming out."

A window popped. Then another. The firemen in Dad's company watched as his grandparents' house became an inferno.

"Baby—" She broke into tears and fell onto the grass.

Bucko stood by him, believing him, as the guilt began to eat Jared alive. His mom had gone in to look for him. His dad had gone in to find his mom.

Jared's hand found the top of his dog's head. Bucko licked him. He looked down at his best bud, tears slipping free. "They're coming out."

Aunt Jilly sobbed harder into the night, and Uncle Brian forced Jared and Bucko away, mixing them with his other cousins who didn't have fathers who were heroes and didn't understand that his parents would walk out of the building.

They were wrapped in blankets, and neighbors fussed to get them inside since they didn't have on shoes. He hadn't even noticed he was barefoot.

Perched in a window of someone's house, Jared couldn't see his grandparents' house anymore. He couldn't tell when his parents walked out. Aunt Margarie made him a drink to ease his mind. Warm milk with a twist, she called it. It made his lips tingle and his tongue feel funny, but as Jared lay on a couch with Bucko and a blanket, he knew that tomorrow hi dad and mom would tell him how they dodged burning fire blasts and jumped over fiery walls. So exciting…he yawned, his head spinning. He'd be a hero one day. Jus like Dad.

CHAPTER 1

Present Day

THE ROOM HUMMED AROUND PARKER Black, and the folder in front of him was so hot a commodity it could burn a hole in his desk. Three new Titan recruits were up for consideration: Jax Riddle, Bishop O'Kane, and Locke Oliver.

Parker could find any information about anyone. He did so for the private sector and the government—United States and its allies. It had been a while since they'd beefed up the team. But at the moment, the dynamic at Titan was solid, and he didn't want to screw it up.

The *click clack* of Sugar's high heels announced her arrival before she entered the room. Lexi, his wife, was in tow, though he couldn't hear her, and the last Parker was told, Sugar needed a final decorative touch for the nursery. Baby Westin would come soon enough. Parker couldn't imagine what a Sugar-Jared nursery woul look like. He was almost scared to see what woul dangle from the baby mobile. And what would the wal decorations be like—pink-and-blue AKs?

Sugar walked in pregnant as all hell, wearing the high heels. "Hey, Boy Genius."

"We're back." Lexi smiled as she sashayed past her best girlfriend and kissed him on the cheek.

"Hey." Parker ran his hand up her back and pulled her in for a better kiss. "Find good stuff?"

"The best."

"Good. Sugar, looking good and gorgeous."

She beamed, her hands resting on her swollen stomach. "What'd you get on the new guys?"

"Sugar!" Lexi's eyebrows bunched.

Sugar shrugged, fidgeting with the cuff of her jacket. "I said we'd find out."

"*Quietly.*" Lexi pressed her lips together, barely containing an eye roll. "We were supposed to be super sly." She turned her smoky-makeup-laden laser focus on him. "But since we're past that point, what do you know so far?"

Parker threw his head back and arms in the air and stretched. "I'm working on it, ladies."

Lexi took advantage of his vulnerable position and slipped onto his lap. "We're snooping nicely."

Sugar crossed her arms, failing to hide her bright-pink smile as she gave him the evil eye. "I'm not."

"Sugar, shut up," Lexi chided.

Parker sucked in a breath. "Easy. Don't upset the delicate, fragile woman with child."

Sugar grabbed one of the chairs in Parker's office, dropped, then spun herself in a circle. She was a sight to see, dressed head to toe in black leather, but she wore a magenta jacket that matched her lipstick. Parker didn't take much notice of fashion, but Sugar was hard to miss.

Lexi, who had a similar-yet-different approach to style, burrowed farther into his lap.

Sugar raised an eyebrow. "Tell us what you got."

Amused, he returned the expression. "This is now a team effort?"

Lexi nodded. "Sugar and I decided that anything you can't hack, her gut will tell us. So if there are holes in your research, we can fill them in."

"Anything I can't hack?" He narrowed his eyes.

"We hurt his feelings," Sugar said.

"Some things require outside-the-office work," Lexi offered. "We are always outside HQ. I could even do some of the heavy lifting on this boring recruit research so you can get back to doing whatever you do. Hack China or crash a drone. Manly stuff."

Sugar sat up, her bright lips forming a devious smile. "It's the perfect combo."

Parker grumbled. "Boss Man benched you, Sugar; you're about to burst."

"*No.* My OB benched me, thank you very much. My husband wouldn't dare."

Lexi kissed Parker's cheek. "I'm between gigs. It's perfect."

"You're buttering me up, and it's not my call." Parker looked at the closed file. He did love working with the ladies. There was no reason to say no. It'd be fun.

His phone rang—the extension coming from Jared's office—and Parker hit the speakerphone. "I got the ladies in here with me."

"Baby Cakes," Jared said as Sugar looked up. "I know what you're up to."

"Good." She beamed. "Less to explain to you at dinner tonight."

"We're not up to anything that you wouldn't already expect." Lexi leaned close to the speakerphone. "However, it's a great idea. Parker and I will do the tech, and Sugar will round out the recruit research with her intuition."

"Yeah, yeah. You know there's more to it than that." Jared grumbled. "You ladies absolutely know that."

They exchanged glances, and at that moment, Parker knew Sugar and Lexi were up to more than they were letting on. He hit the mute button. "Whoa. Hang on."

Both smiled so big and fake that he dropped his head back. "Shit, I don't want to know."

"Parker, do you want the help?" Jared asked. "Hello? Am I talking to myself here?"

He gave Lexi *the* look and then Sugar a version of it as well. "You have one hour to go tell Jared whatever the hell you are up to, and you, darling dearest"—he squeezed Lexi—"will fess up in ten minutes."

Lexi giggled—a dead giveaway.

"Brother." He hit the unmute button. "Yeah. I'll take Lexi's help." He wrapped his arms around his wife's shoulders, taking any excuse to hang out and work with her simultaneously. "That works for me. Sugar's headed your way; she has something to run by you first, though."

Sugar pointed her fingers at him, pretending to shoot, and Parker tossed a pen, ignoring her antics.

"Fine. Done," Jared said. "See you in five, Baby Cakes."

The phone's line went out, and Sugar pushed herself out of the spinning chair with dramatic flair. "Buzz kill, Boy Genius."

"Out." He grinned.

"It's more fun to make him work for it."

"Maybe for you, Sugar."

She winked. "Always for me."

Soon as the door shut, he turned Lexi in his lap so

she couldn't look anywhere but at him. "Spit it out."

Her smile reached her ears. "New recruits have the interviews."

"Yeah."

"The background checks."

He nodded. "Yes."

"They're…under surveillance."

Surveillance. Sugar might have had field training but Lexi had not. She was a loner, a hacker, and had survived more than her fair share of harrowing situations. Parker preferred that she stay far from anyone who could possibly be worthy of surveillance. "Nope."

Determination flashed on her face. "It's not like we're going to go watch people who are actually bad guys. They're the good guys, just wandering around without a job—"

"They have jobs. Deadly jobs."

"Well, not at home they don't."

"Lex." *Christ.*

"We'll just stay in the car or whatever. Give us some of that Titan gear you guys hang on to, and we can see through the wall." She winked. "Come on. Sugar's going nuts. She's not the type to nest."

"Nest?"

His wife smiled but rolled her lips as though she wanted to hide it. "It's almost time for Sugar to give birth. Some women in her position *nest.* They clean the house top to bottom. They have uncontrollable rges to prepare their home for the new arrival."

He smirked, now knowing why Lexi hid her smile. A ridiculous image of Sugar scrubbing the rafters in leather maternity pants came to mind. "I'm sure the Vestins have a top-secret-cleared cleaning staff proficient in the art of *nesting*."

Lexi's not-so-hidden smile came out in full force. "You're missing my point. It's her last hurrah. And it's safe. We'll behave. Sugar wants a road trip, *and* what she said is true. She has an instinct that Titan relies on. The girl could pick a bad apple out of an orchard. Bad bullet out of a barrel. Whatever. Let her help vet the new recruits."

Parker shook his head.

Lexi pursed her lips. "It'll be a piece of cake."

No way would Jared allow Sugar, eight months pregnant, to search out the potential new team members and go undercover to watch their every move. "There's not a chance that will fly."

Her eyes narrowed. "Well, we're going to do it."

"You, maybe. He'll give the okay to let you hack some data. But Sugar in the field? Nope."

"We're going to do it." Lexi's statement sounded like a practiced mantra.

"Lex—"

"Sugar and I are going on a pre-baby, nondangerous, surveillance-only road trip!" She smacked him with a kiss. "And it's going to be *awesome*."

"This wasn't really a discussion, was it?"

She kissed him again. "No, babe. It wasn't."

At least he'd tried. Then again…he wondered how Jared was taking the news from Sugar.

CHAPTER 2

F THERE WAS A TELLTALE sign that trouble was about to show up at Jared's office doorstep, it was the cadence of Sugar's step and the corresponding groan of his dog, Thelma. Sugar marched in, her posture and expression telling him she was sure that she'd get her way and that he had major reason to be concerned. Thelma placed a short, stubby paw over her wrinkly bulldog face and rolled over at his boots.

He leaned back in his chair. "This oughta be good."

"Always is." She leaned against the doorframe, looking hotter than the Fourth of July. Her smile said, *Just try me*, and her eyes dared him to disagree. The challenge she had yet to issue had him aroused, and attitude alone had him horny as all hell and wanting to push out of his chair and press her against the wall. This was their game, and damn, he loved it.

She tilted her head, letting her dark hair fall ov
her shoulder. "You're looking particularly studl
over there. Doing big, important things today, Bos
Man?"

"Breaking out the *Boss Man*, huh?" He grumble
and laughed, rocking back in his chair, and watched he
sway her hips forward as she walked like sex an
stealth swirled into one.

His wife was a smokin' sex goddess even pregnant
Too bad she knew it and would use those fuck-me eye
and screw him senseless until she got whatever answe
she wanted.

Sugar sat her leather-clad hip on the edge of hi
desk, and they locked their gazes. "Thelma, honey. G
in the next room. There's a treat."

"Ruthless." His pulse jumped. Kicking the do
out meant Sugar wanted her way, and it almos
always meant her sweet pussy was his for the taking
No one would dare walk into his office withou
permission, and if his wife wanted to play th
seductress, Jared would have zero complaints o
accidental voyeurs.

"What?" She scooted closer to him on the desk
"Don't you want to play with me?"

"If you think"—he pulled her leg so that she sat ir
front of him, straddling his chair—"that this wil
change whatever I have to say, Baby Cakes, you'r
mistaken."

"Pity." She smirked but leaned close enough that he could smell her shampoo. "Kiss me anyway, and let's see how it goes."

She didn't wait for an answer, and her mouth tasted bubble-gum sweet. His hands rested on her thighs, his tongue tangled in her mouth as her fingernails scratched the back of his scalp.

"The places I want your tongue. Care to guess?" she purred into his kiss.

Damn. She'd likely get whatever she wanted. He inched forward, licking the delicious slope of her neck. He stifled his own groan and kissed the soft skin. "Here."

"I won't complain."

"Woman…"

She murmured in a way that was a stroke to his shaft.

His tongue ran behind her ear. "You like this."

"Mm-hmm." Sugar shifted on the desk, a quiet gasp giving her away.

"You love it." He upped his game and scraped his teeth against her, nibbling as she tried to hold the upper hand.

"I love a lot of things you do to me."

He pulled back, not giving in to her games so easily. "You're up to no good."

God. Sexy sat in front of him. Flushed cheeks, heavy eyelids. Her lips were parted, and her hair was a

mess. He hadn't even started with that yet. "Yes," sh
said.

"You're going stir crazy. I've been watching you."

She nodded, gaze set on his. "Yes, sir."

He rewarded her with the slightest of smiles fo
breaking out the big guns with the *sir*. "You want a
job?"

"Not exactly." Sugar's dark-blue eyes intensified.

"Then what?"

She put her palms flat on his chest then raked he
fingers down. "Sex first, business later?"

Jared ran both hands down her thigh, answering he
without a word, and unzipped the knee-high boot
tugging it free. He stripped the sock and held her bare
foot in his hand, running his thumb along the arch
"Whatever it is, you'll be careful."

Her head dropped back. "Mm-hmm."

"Good girl." He worked his way down the sole
of her foot, watching her squirm as he changed the
pressure. His thumbs worked her heel and pressed
deep circles, sliding to her ankles, then flexing he
foot back until he massaged her brightly painted
toes.

"God, that's insane," she whispered.

He took the other boot off, repeating the process
watching her melt. "You came into my office
planning to take over, and look what happened
Sugar."

She bit her lip and let her hair tumble forward. This was my plan. For you to take over, J-dawg. And you know it."

Either way, at that point, he didn't care. "Stand up."

With a lazy, sexed-up smile, she stood, and he pulled her pants right off. After months of trying to figure out what was easiest—and Sugar insisted on maintaining her *look* in maternity wear—Jared had determined that to get his wife out of leather maternity pants in a reasonable amount of time, he needed to be part of the process.

She laughed. "Greedy."

"Hungry." He unfastened his belt. "For you."

"Good." There was nothing sexier than her flushed cheeks when Sugar was set on making him feel good.

He moved closer to the edge of his chair. "Turn around."

"You just want to see my ass."

Hell yeah, he did. But he wanted to wrap his arms around his woman, wanted to feel his cock deep inside her, and Sugar sitting backwards on his lap would do that for him. Jared playfully smacked her butt as she turned around. "It's a great ass."

She stuck it out, and he squeezed her cheeks then let his hands drift down her thighs, spreading his fingers over the silken flesh of her legs. One hand went up, running over her heavy, pregnant-with-his-child belly and the other stopped between her thighs, finding her folds wet. One touch, and she shifted, sucking a deep breath.

"Too much?" He slowed.

"Not at all." Sugar moved for him again, leaning her weight against his touch.

Jared stroked the delicate, sensitive area and watched how her back arched. His forefinger opened her, and she moaned. "Good, baby?"

She nodded, letting the cascade of dark hair falling down her back mesmerize him. How could his woman so brash and biting, so sexy and sultry, simply shake her hair without looking his way and have him damn near do anything to make her happy?

Jared massaged her clit with one hand, breaching her pussy with the fingers of his other.

Her hips flexed, grinding on his palm, riding for more friction. "Please, Jared."

That was all he needed. "Damn." She inched and angled her body, and he slid his pants down to his boots. His erection was free and in hand. Sugar turned her head, peering at him over her shoulder.

"You ready?" he asked.

She nodded. "If you don't hurry up—"

His woman. He would've spent more time trying to aggravate her, except he was dying to be inside her body. Positioning the head of his shaft and—goddamn ared's molars ground down. Sugar's tight pussy would ill him. "Shit, Baby Cakes."

Together, their breathing caught. Sugar's hands played on his desk as she inched back onto his cock, nd he couldn't handle another moment. He thrust. Her ails scratched, unable to find traction on the finished vood. "Fuck, yes. Jared. *Yes.*"

He couldn't breathe. She leaned back, her hips noving up, down, accommodating him, and he roaned, flexing, wrangling his arms around her to hold er in place. Sugar held on to him. Her arms were a vise rip, holding on as though he were a life raft.

"Again." Her whisper boomed to the base of his ock.

He flexed up.

"God," she gasped.

"Good?" He grunted.

"Yes."

"Good." He did it again. Short. Rapid. Bursts. He ossessed his wife—holding her, letting her feel every ingle fucking inch of his cock inside her body.

"More," she begged.

Sugar consumed his shaft. He controlled her, wned her, moved her up and down, the silken eeling of her slickness working tighter and hungrier s he drove. The sound of their gasps comingled. iery electricity flowed down his spine, drawing his alls tight.

Her head went down. Her teeth—he felt them bit into him somewhere. *God*, she had his flesh between her teeth, but all he knew was that her pussy muscle rippled.

Sugar bore down on him, using his hold as a fulcrum, and her orgasm hit them both—a complete supernova, its intensity blinding. Her body milked his pulsing cock, and his hot release was an act o heaven.

Sugar went limp in his hug, kissing his arm— where apparently she had bitten him—and he chest heaved. "You sure know how to show who': boss."

He chortled, shaking his head languidly. "Damn you are fun."

"To love, to fuck, to hold," she whispered. "To work with."

She stood carefully and turned, and he couldn't help but admire the pink in her cheeks that didn't come from makeup. Her lips were pinker than her lipstick and her eyes more blue than when she'd first walked into his office. He did that to her. That left a mark of pride in his chest.

"Prove you love me, and help slide those pants back on me." She winked. "I can't convince you of my grea plan when I'm half-naked."

He snagged the leather pants and underwear off the floor. "You might not convince me anyway." But tha was a lie. She didn't need to convince him, and he wouldn't stop her.

"Like I need your permission." She snagged the black panties and hopped as best she could from one foot to the next while he pulled up his pants and tucked himself in. "But I want it."

That was why they worked in sync. There hadn't been a job in a very long time that Jared hadn't run by Sugar. She had the mind of an operator and the discerning ability to figure out how to blow shit up in a way that flat-out impressed him. And turned him on. Great combination in a wife.

"Elevator pitch. Let's hear it." He smoothed his shirt and adjusted his pants so that only they would know he'd just been well fucked.

"You have three wannabe new guys. Lexi and I want to be the team that does the on-the-ground observation."

He blinked, surprised. "You want to do the surveillance?"

"Yes."

"That's boring as shit." So where was the catch?

She raised an eyebrow.

Well, nothing was boring as shit when Sugar was involved. "If you do it, you have to stay out of the fray. Away from the newbies. Watch and report. That's it."

Kiss-swollen lips smiled as if she had her *yes* already. "We can do that."

"From *afar*, Sugar."

"No kidding."

"Meaning, you can't interact with them, babe. Read me?"

She smirked. "No shit, J-dawg."

"You can't bump into them." He ticked off one finger.

"I'm not stupid."

He ticked off another finger. "You can't do whatever it is you're thinking about."

She narrowed her gaze. "Yes, I can."

"God, woman." He closed his fist, not bothering to count off the dozens of other things she shouldn't do. "You give me heartburn."

"No. Those are orgasms I give you, baby."

Jared dropped his head back and roared. "Damn straight, pretty mama. You do what you need to." But he sobered and rubbed a hand over his face, feeling the strain of laughter in his cheeks. "But no shit, Sugar. You, Asal, and this baby? My world. You've never asked me to change; I'll never ask you to either. If you need to get out there, go. If something makes you feel uncomfortable, don't for a moment hesitate to flag for help because you're worried I'll be pissed you're in the field. You read me?"

"I do."

"Unconditional trust."

Her eyes went watery. "Fucking hormones."

28

"So you read me?" he said again, quieter this time.

"Loud and clear, Boss Man." She leaned forward and placed a sweetly gentle kiss on his lips. "And I love you too."

CHAPTER 3

THE HOUSE WAS QUIET AS Parker and Lexi sat around their dining-room table, three recruit folders spread in front of them.

Bishop O'Kane. Jax Riddle. Locke Oliver.

"They're all insanely…" Lexi gestured, staring at the screen of her laptop. "Deadly?"

Parker didn't look up from his screen. "That's a good thing, babe."

"Right. And they're clean enough."

He nodded. The records showed skirmishes here and there—nothing that couldn't be expected from men who operated at the caliber of Titan's people.

"Your ice cream's melting," she said. "And I need another beer if we're going to stare at the same data all night."

"No." He pushed his chair from the table and stretched as he stood. "Come on. We're done."

"Jax and Locke are too far away."

"Right," he agreed. Locke worked private ops i
London, and Jax was on the West Coast. Titan coul
drop someone in to do the recon on them in person. N
need for the Sugar-Lexi road trip to go trans-Atlantic o
cross-country.

"So Bishop's our guy."

Parker wrapped his arms around her chest, pressin
her back to him, leading her to the couch. "Bishop'
your guy. Be easy on him." He kissed her cheek. "An
by *be easy*, I mean don't do anything."

"I know. But still, this is exciting."

He plopped them both down, and Lexi curled int
his arms while he surfed the channels for somethin
sports related. With a football-classics channel on in th
background, he tied her hair around his finger an
watched her smoky eyes flutter open and closed. "S
exciting, you're falling asleep."

"Stop it." She turned in the crook of his arm. "Yo
get to play cops and robbers all the time. Sugar does
Everyone does. I think it's neat even if I just get to sit i
a car and listen to my girl babble about her spot-on gu
feeling. It's something different."

Parker pressed a kiss to the top of her head. "Just b
careful."

"How much trouble can we get into watching a gu
grocery shop or whatever?"

His rumbling laugh met hers. With Sugar, they both knew the answer.

"Alright. Of course we'll be careful."

"Good." He let go of a piece of her platinum-blond hair. "Go to sleep, and I'll carry you to bed."

Lexi turned over on her chest. "Why am I going to sleep?"

"Uh…sports? Because your eyes are shut?"

"I'm a full-fledged spy girl now."

"Alright, spy girl. You don't need to sleep."

"Maybe I do. Either way, I know this isn't technically how you guys scout your new team members. But really, Sugar was going stir-crazy. She needed to feel as though she was still important to your team."

"Of course she is."

"I just kind of *know* that there's something unexplainable about being pregnant and having folks handle you with kid gloves. It has to be a first for her."

He cackled. "No one's treating her any different."

"Bull. Even Sugar's treating herself different."

Parker squeezed Lexi tight. "We take care of our own."

As she snuggled into his chest, her previous life seemed a thousand miles away, yet she knew he was dead serious. "I love you, and I love being part of your world."

"It's not just this job, Lex. Or what you do for Jared

behind a computer screen." He kissed the top of he head. "You are our world. Once you're in, you're in Titan for life."

———————

PARKER AND JARED HAD THEIR arms crossed over their chests as Sugar inspected the last bag they'd packed into her Range Rover. "Alrighty, boys. Don't worry."

"Famous last words," Jared grumbled.

"Do you feel like all we've been saying and hearing is *Don't worry*?" Parker added, eyeing Jared and, from Sugar's vantage point, possibly antagonizing him on purpose.

"Seriously." Sugar gave Parker the stink eye then raised her eyebrow at her husband. "You're acting like I can't do anything because I'm pregnant."

Jared took a boot-cladded step forward. "No."

"Yes."

"Kind of," Lexi said. "Super-protective, alpha-to-the-max Jared. We get it. But—"

"I've literally packed gummy bears to snack on." Sugar matched Jared's step forward. "No extra ammo—"

"You've packed *any* ammo?" He took another step forward as though he was ready to search her Range Rover.

"No. Well, other than what I'd obviously conceal nd carry."

His eyes narrowed. "Do you have anything high-owered or automatic in there?"

God, he was fun to torque. Sugar popped a bubble f gum. "Define high-powered."

"Christ, Sugar."

"I'm kidding. Calm down. No C4. No AKs. We're ine." She turned for the driver's door, listening to the rumbling, cursing man of steel behind her. "Come on, ex. Let's rock and roll."

"Woman." Jared growled. "Get your sweet ass over ere and kiss me good-bye."

That was what Sugar was waiting for. She all but kipped over to Jared and wrapped her arms around his eck. "I love you. I promise I won't do anything that ets us into a pickle."

"I know." His hand rested on her stomach. Even vhen he was sour and scratchy, Jared was the epitome f soft—until provoked—when it came to their hildren. "You and this baby stay safe. Hear me?"

"Yeah, Boss Man." She winked and gave him a kiss ecause he was a pain in the ass, because he was *her* ain in the ass, and because his mister-bossy-pants act vas endearing and made her love him even more each nd every day. "Remember how much I'm irritating the iss out of you."

"How could I forget?"

"You can't." She bobbed her eyebrows. "But I' like you to remind me of just how bad I'm being later i bed. Capiche?"

His eyes darkened, and she smacked a kiss on hi lips again.

"So much fun." She scraped her nails down hi chest. "I almost hate to leave."

"Stop messing with him, Sugar," Lexi called. She was already in the passenger seat.

Sugar dropped her hands on top of Jared's the squeezed. "Guess I can do that."

He smiled, and it lit her world. "Stay safe, baby."

"I can do that too." Sugar gave him one more kis and moved behind the steering wheel.

"You ladies good?" Parker asked, keeping eyes o Lexi.

"Always," Lexi said sweetly.

Sugar shook her head. "If you messed with Bo Genius more, you might get lai—"

"Don't push yourself too hard, alright, Sugar? Parker laughed then waved bye to them both afte kissing Lexi once more. "Stay safe."

He shut the door then rapped on the SUV's roo twice. The garage door from Titan HQ's undergroun basement started to lift, and Sugar's blood surged. I might not be the wild ride their husbands were scare they might go on, but it was a last hurrah before she ha to buckle down with a newborn.

Slipping a new piece of gum into her mouth, Sugar lowered her sunglasses as Lexi did the same. They exchanged looks, Sugar revved the gas just to irritate Jared, then they left Titan with a GPS filled with a plan and likely a tracking device on their vehicle. It didn't matter. For the moment, Sugar felt free.

———————

WATCHING SUGAR ROLL OUT OF Titan HQ was a normal occurrence. But this time, his gut churned, and the overprotective vibe that he always had—and that he had to keep semi-in-check because the woman could hold her own—was on full blast.

Jared stretched and rubbed the back of his neck. What was the root cause? The due date ticked closer. Maybe that was it.

He had Asal. It wasn't as if he was a first-time father-to-be.

But in a way, yeah, he was. An actual baby in the house was akin to a new chapter in his life, and while he was ready for that, it meant change.

Change wasn't something he craved. Stability, permanence, solidness—those were the foundations on which he'd built his life. Order was established. Things had a reason for happening and a way in which they were conducted.

Yet he couldn't be more excited. Yesterday Sugar had been blabbing on and on to some of the girls at GUNS, her gun shop and range, about how they were having a little girl. He couldn't help but smile.

A year ago, if someone had shown him pink camo, he would've asked, "Where are they hiding? Candy land?" Now that shit was cute. Asal wasn't into the pink camo. His big girl liked her real-life camo.

But a little baby bundle in his woman's arms? Yeah, it'd work just as much as his newborn girl would look good in the pink Harley Davidson outfits, which he also bought. Maybe he wouldn't bring a newborn to Sturgis. But a little one at Sturgis? Hell yeah. Asal loved it. Sugar loved it. Why not make it a Westin family tradition?

That hit him in the chest. Maybe it was already a family tradition. They'd made their own, and new ones would come. He tugged his lip into his mouth, rolling that thought over.

"Are you that worried?" Parker interrupted his thoughts, reading him all wrong.

"Just thinking."

"About?"

Jared cleared his throat and mind. "Take your pick. The trouble Sugar'll wriggle into. The headaches she'll leave along the way." He chuckled. "Want me to go on?"

Parker shook his head. "Lexi will keep her grounded."

"Glad they've become such good friends."

"Me too," Jared mumbled. "Has Sugar had Lexi down at the range?"

"Not much. It's not her thing."

"Right." He wondered how someone would fall in love with anyone in Titan and not understand who they were and how they got there. Weapons were a part of that, but it was so much more than handling a gun. It was their lifestyle. For Sugar and Lexi to gel the way they had…he'd have to ask Sugar about it. She didn't take on anyone that she didn't know everything about. Jared pinched the bridge of his nose and remembered one of the first times he'd slept over at Sugar's house. "So how does a big, bossy, badass of a man decide to go into the army?" Sugar had lain naked across his chest.

"You want all my secrets?"

"I want everything from you. I didn't mention that?"

He ran his hands down her bare back and let his palms rest on her ass. "I needed a job. They'd be stupid not to take me. End of story."

"Bull-fucking-shit."

He'd squeezed her ass. "You think you know me so well."

"I do. But I want all of you. Every last piece of intel. What makes you tick?" Sugar had let the minutes drift by. "This will never work unless you let me in And the reason Jared Westin is the man he is has something major to do with why you signed up for someone to hand you a gun."

Jared remembered wanting to fight her, shake her Run but also stay put. "Sugar…"

"Your call, buddy. I can roll with it either way. I'm a big girl. We've established that."

Minutes had passed, and he had no intention of letting Sugar get away. But as for the past and who he was, there wasn't much to say. Just a series of facts and events, and here he was—Army Ranger turned Titan Group founder and lucky as hell to have her in bed.

"Spit it out." She had shifted away, and he'd snagged her back.

"Stay put."

"Start talking."

"It comes down to one thing. I grew up believing in heroes." He'd taken a deep breath and wrapped her into a hug, sliding her body next to him so they were eye to eye. "Some people will do anything to save another person. Some people would rather drop and cry about tragedy."

"True. But that's vague."

He'd smiled because only the woman he'd spend the rest of his life with would call him out as he tried to verbalize feelings and pivotal life points. "My grandfather had dementia. I don't know what they

alled it back then. My grandma, just…maybe had
nough. All of the family was over at their place for
Christmas, and he didn't remember a thing. No one.
Not her."

"That's awful."

"But it turns out she locked the door, lit a cigarette,
nd went to sleep. I'm not sure how she killed him,
illed herself…" It would have ruined his childhood if
e hadn't been as strong of a kid as he was. "I saw my
unts and uncles drop to their knees and cry. I saw
eople walk away. But my parents were heroes. And
when the time came for me to make a decision, it
wasn't about putting a gun in my hand; it was about
who best could push me to be like them."

"Still too simple."

All of that, and it hadn't been enough. He wanted to
augh. "What are you, a therapist?"

Sugar had smiled. The woman had a thousand
xpressions that all seemed to boil down to how she
moved her lips. "For the purposes of this conversation,
ou call me whatever you want, Boss Man."

"The fire changed my world view. I thought
veryone lived a certain way. Followed orders.
Understood chain of command. I was wrong, and I
wanted to associate only with those who did. I wanted
o honor those who would lay down their lives for me. I
wanted to be invincible like my dad and as selfless as
my mom. I wanted to be an Army Ranger."

41

Jared took a deep breath, pulling himself from th
flashback. If he and Sugar could be a tenth of th
parents his folks were, they'd be doing something right

"Alright, I'm headed in to monitor the Delta team'
transmissions." Parker left, his steps echoing in th
garage.

Jared cracked his knuckles and waited for Sugar'
first update, missing her already. He pulled out his cel
phone and sent a text to Asal just because. He wa
following Parker's path toward the secure door whe
his phone buzzed. He swiped the screen. His daughte
sent a selfie: one eye closed, the other squinting. He
tongue was out, and one side of her face was squashed
with her hand. The text overlay said, "Beat that!"

He laughed, made a better face, then snapped th
selfie and sent it back to his daughter with the hashtag
"#dadwins."

CHAPTER 4

THE SCENT OF PANCAKES AND syrup filled the air.
There were enough blue-haired Betties catching glances
at the Lexi and Sugar partnership that Lexi had to chew
the inside of her mouth not to smile and wave. The start
of this road trip was entertaining for everyone—for her
and Sugar and the people who didn't generally see
people like…well, Sugar, on a daily basis.

"So he's a meathead?" Sugar stabbed a Nutella-
covered crepe. "His schedule for the last week, outside
of work, is: the gym, the vitamin place, the place where
he picks up his food, and the gym."

Lexi rolled the cooling coffee cup back and forth
between her fingers. "He's got a stack of
commendations and crap on his résumé. Shouldn't you
know more about that?"

"That crap doesn't impress me." Sugar took another
bite.

"Well, obviously me either. I searched throug every electronic fingerprint I could find. Squeaky-clea outside of military activities. Typical Titan." Lexi tool a sip. "So we remain wholly unimpressed. Great résumé and a meathead schedule. A few headshots that are a generic as the rest of his stellar military career Hoorah."

"*Hooah.* The army says, *hooah.*"

"See." Lexi traded her coffee cup for a fork an went to town on her hash browns. "I have no idea. Th vitamin store would be the best place for us to go. W can wander around, maybe see if he's a jackass."

"Why the vitamin store?"

"You're pregnant and all. Vitamins? Hello?"

Sugar shook her head. "They're prescription. M OB calls those horse pills in."

"Oh." Lexi shrugged. "Clueless in the pregg department."

"We should go to the gym."

"Ha!" Lexi snorted. "Oh, wait. Are you serious?"

"Sure." Sugar shrugged and smirked. "Why not I'm supposed to get some exercise."

"Have you ever been inside a gym?"

Her face tightened. "I was ATF. I'm a trained killer thank you very much, little miss keyboards and leather I have been inside a gym."

"That's not what I meant." Lexi searched for th right words. "This gym seems different. More tha

44

where dudes just pump iron all day. This is more like the kind of gym where they just find things that are heavy and… I don't know, hold them. Throw them. Lift them. Then take selfies."

Sugar laughed. "Like at all gyms."

"This isn't like where you get a flyer in the mail to join for a month for free. This is where they pick up tractor tires or something and grunt a lot."

"We might stick out." Sugar tapped a manicured fingernail.

Lexi laughed. "Ya think?"

"So we go shopping."

"I don't know if we can tone down the amount of awesome between the two of us."

Sugar's eyes scrutinized her own clothes then Lexi's. "Well, we do look amazing and all, seeing as everyone in Mayberry's finest pancake shop can't take their eyes off of us, but blending in is another thing."

Lexi's eyebrow went up. "We need badass gym clothes."

"Yeah, we do. Might not do the trick, but at least it will get us through the door."

"This isn't at all what Jared had in mind." Lexi bit her lip, thinking back to the lecture about how this was essentially her first time in the field on Titan's schedule and she had to follow certain rules, none of which Sugar was allowed to trump.

"Jared's rules boiled down to this: don't get hurt,

and don't put the baby in a bad position. We're going to a gym. It's literally on the list of activities I'm supposed to do—get exercise."

Lexi sipped her coffee. "Just so you know, I'm not getting into it with you two."

"You don't have to. It's great sex when we fight. If something causes a problem with Jared, great things happen, and I'd never actually do anything that would put the baby at risk."

Lexi's face pinched. "Ew. More than I needed to know."

Sugar pulled a pen from her purse and grabbed a napkin. "Shopping list time. Do we need new iPods?" She paused. "Clothes, new shoes…what else? Snacks. Hmmm."

"Definitely some of those chocolate-coconut bars we finished off on the way up here."

Sugar nodded.

"Surveillance work is great. Remind me to tell Parker to shove it next time he complains."

Sugar penned *SNACKS* and circled it. "Ten-four, buckaroo. Time to get our workout on."

―――――――――

THE RHYTHMIC POUNDING OF THE man running for his life in between Sugar's and Lexi's treadmills was more an enough up-close proof that Bishop O'Kane was as physically fit as his profile said. This gym catered to professional bodybuilders but was empty with the exception of one other person and staff. It was elite and niche, and Sugar had basically used her stomach and her hormones to get them a day pass.

Not exactly Titan-level detective work, but this was more a girl's trip than anything else...right? Her phone buzzed as she and Lexi walked lazily on either side of their unknowing target.

Lexi: *What have we learned? I'm bored.*
Sugar: *I was bored at home. This was*
something to do.
Lexi: *Right.*
Lexi: *I think he knows we know each other.*
Lexi: *Shit! He's looking at both of us.*
Lexi: *SUGAR!*

Sugar got off her treadmill and walked calmly to the bathroom. The second she was out of sight, she pulled her phone back out.

Sugar: *Do I have to teach you how to creep up*
on a dude!?!?
Lexi: *Maybe...*

She tittered to herself. Well, that was probably true.

For as hot as Lexi was, she was clueless when it came to the art of flirting. Though they weren't flirting. But still, spying on a guy took a certain level of finesse that Lexi didn't have.

> Sugar: *We need a new game plan.*
> Sugar: *Does he still look suspicious of us?*
> Sugar: *Hello?*
> Sugar: *Hey, Thelma, it's Louise. Why'd you go radio silent?*
> Lexi: *We have a problem*
> Sugar: *On a scale of 1 to 10, 1 is we need to hit the pancake house again, and 10 is I have to hit up GUNS for the ammo Jared wouldn't let me have, gimme a number.*

She grabbed her bag from a locker and wrestled out of her exercise pants and back into leather pants, which—thank the Lord for maternity adaptation—were more comfortable.

Sugar's screen blinked with the text.

> Lexi: *10. 10. 10.*
> Sugar: *Easy, killer. On my way.*

But the text wouldn't send. The little circle kept circling. No signal. Ugh. *What the hell?* She pushed out the door to find the hallway dark. A tickle of adrenaline rept up her neck, and she slowed her pace.

"Hello?" A Russian accent called into the bathroom where she had just been.

Training and instinct made Sugar drop to the floor, listening to the voice continue to call and the person go in and out of the locker rooms and whatever rooms were down the other hallway.

Her pulse picked up. She could feel the blood pumping in her neck and in her *stomach*, which was a change from the norm. But all in all, this was no different than creeping like a shadow on any other job. Except she didn't know who or what she was dealing with, and she had to hide what felt like an additional few feet of her stomach from view while trying to figure out what the double deuces was happening.

She tried her cell phone again. *Shit.* She got nothing but a spinning circle and a *no service* signal. Clearly, somewhere in the building was a cell-phone jammer, which meant this was more of a professional job than a slam-and-bam robbery.

Okay…what to do?

Slinking down the hallway, she heard no exercise equipment clinking and clanking. No men throwing heavy things. No people grunting as they lifted heavy objects for personal enjoyment. There was only the empty blare of music that, now that all was abandoned and quiet, played far too loud. Her phone continued to cycle without a signal, and Sugar's eyes searched for signs of anyone in the building—most importantly Lexi. And where had that searching Russian man gone She needed a weapon. Fast.

She checked her phone again.

Nope. *The hell with it.* She tucked it in her back pocket. Across the open floor were hand weights. She could grab a few jump ropes or one of the calisthenic bars while she was there. But crossing the gym was too dangerous. With a view of nothing but treadmills elliptical machines, and stair climbers, she had nothing but magazines to smack a bad dude with. Nothing deadly.

So the plan for the moment was to keep against the wall and head for the main desk. Surely there was a pair of scissors. A stapler. Hell, she could be deadly with a phone cord. All she needed was the right angle. But really, Sugar stressed about Lexi.

She crept around another corner of the main gym No one was there.

No Lexi. No Bishop. No random meatheads. No guy with a Russian accent searching for rogue people hiding and creeping.

"What the fuckballs?" Her pulse pounded in her neck, and confusion covered every thought. Only Emergency Exit signs illuminated the room, and the place was eerie as shit.

Her quiet question went unanswered, and the baby took that moment to kick. "Easy, tater tot. I've got this."

Creeping quiet as a mofo, Sugar found her way to the front desk where they'd checked in. Gone was the buff little dude who all but made her swear her life away for a one-day pass. She lifted the phone. No dial tone. The computer was off. There was no electricity of any kind. Sugar popped the cord from the receiver and base, winding it in her hand then tucking it into the sleeve of her shirt. She had no idea when or how that would come in handy, but at least she had something.

And she wanted a stapler. Where was a damn stapler? What kind of front desk didn't have a stapler? But scissors she found. Sugar tucked those into her sock.

She tried to think of what other pseudo weapons could she kill someone with. Tapping her manicured fingers on the desk, keeping careful eyes out, she snagged a handful of paper clips and shoved them in her back pocket, having no freakin' clue what she planned to do with those babies, but whatever—they had sharp, pokey edges.

The front door was open, but she didn't have another way to call for help. Maybe she should leave and go drive for help. But what would she say—that the lights were out and her friend was gone?

Well, yeah.

But what the hell was going on?

The baby kicked her stomach. Hard. Alright—she had to be smart about this. Yeah, she'd been a kick-ass

ATF agent at one point, and then Titan had trained her to be better than she could ever imagine.

But the child-on-the-way thing was a complication, at least in the badass, ass-kicking department. *Go get help.* That was the only option. She tucked away her pride and carefully ducked and maneuvered for the front exit. Her eyes searched everywhere, and her ears listened for any sound that could lay claim to danger.

Click.

There were few sounds that could make Sugar stop and freeze. The flick of a safety on a gun was one. She didn't move, didn't breathe. The fucker didn't have to order her not to move. Waiting took forever and made her seethe more than it made her fear.

"Turn around." Finally, the asshole gave her a chance.

She turned.

Bishop O'Kane?

"What the fuck?" she hissed. "Get that out of my face."

Other than one eyebrow twitching at what had to be surprise, he didn't move. "Shoving Glocks in pregnant ladies' faces isn't my favorite thing. If you're not part of my problem, good. If you are part of this mess, I don't care who, how, or what you are, lady."

She grinned and instinctually made her decision. This guy would work for Titan.

"Wipe the smirk off your face. Sit down." He

nwound one of the jump ropes from his side and irected her to the chair at the front desk. "You'll stay ut until I figure out—"

"First, I'm pregnant, not a pariah. You should still at me down. You have no clue if this"—she tapped her rotruding tummy—"is even real. Or what I'm acking."

Bishop blinked. "Excuse me? What is this, lessons n the field by the lady in leather?" He shook his head, ut he *did* go about patting her down.

"Phone cord?" He held it up, unbelieving.

She shrugged. "Limited resources."

He checked her stomach, determining in the most wkward of ways that it was, in fact, not a fake tomach—most notably, when her stomach twitched nd he jumped. She snickered, and he smirked, running is hands to her shoes, finding the scissors, and lisarming her with a look that said he was seriously uestioning her sanity.

"What? The lights went out. No one was around."

He turned her around and found the stash of paper lips and cell phone, placing them both on the desk. "What are you? The pregnant MacGyver?"

"Best compliment I've had in a while."

"Sit down," he ordered, unamused.

Complying, Sugar realized she should have peed efore all this started. That kind of request was likely to all on deaf ears, and the timing was really bad.

"I've got shit to do. Don't need this from a gym rat." He bound a wrist to the chair, reached around, and started on the other. "Please sit down and be quiet. You'll stay safe and out of the way."

"Ouch." She winced, putting her acting skills on display.

Bishop drew back an inch, inspecting his rope work. "Bullshit."

"I'm *pregnant*."

His eyes dropped to her stomach as though he hadn't confirmed that two seconds ago. "Are you serious? Do you understand that I need you to shut your mouth? You had a gun to your head. I'm tying you to a chair. You're in danger. I'm your ticket out of here. Please be quiet. Can you do that for me?"

This guy was great. "Don't be nice to me. I could still be the enemy."

"Jesus. Who the hell are you?" he mumbled, continuing to wrap her wrist. He tested it, she noted, not only to see that she couldn't get out but that it didn't hurt her wrist.

"So what's going on? Seeing as you just tied up an innocent bystander."

"Stay put. Don't move. If you're not involved, you'll be home in time for dinner. Deal?"

Screwing with him and judging his handiwork for a Titan-recruit file aside, this was not a great situation. Lexi had no idea how to handle herself in the field, and ugar didn't like being out of the loop. "Wait, okay. Vait. For real, what's going on?"

"Stay put."

"My name is Sugar."

"Great—"

"My girl's name is Lexi."

"Fine."

"She's married to Parker Black. This little to-be-orn bundle of joy"—Sugar tilted her head toward her tomach—"belongs to Jared Westin."

Bishop's face showed ten thousand emotions in ero-point-two seconds. "*Fuck.*" In three steps, he was n her, unbinding her and rubbing her arms. "Why the ell didn't you say something?"

"I'm a sadistic bitch who was on her way to go get ome kind of help. A first for me since I'd much rather now whatever it is that you're about to do."

"I cannot believe this." Tension flexed in his jaw. Jared Westin's *pregnant* wife and Russian gangsters. I id not sign up for this shit."

"Well, I didn't either—actually, I did."

He lifted an eyebrow.

"You're on a short list. We're checking you out. I ilked my way onto your surveillance team."

"Duck down here." He pushed her under a desk. There's a reason surveillance stays in cars."

She winked. "Ah, the student schools the teacher."

"Christ." He grumbled, still amused.

"So Lexi?" she asked.

"She's fine. Everyone here's in a separate room."

"You're not?"

"Yeah, call me Superman. And I need to go d something about that before they realize I'm gone Look, I told a buddy I'd watch a job for him."

"This is the job?" she asked.

Bishop nodded. "Looks like a deal's going dow early, and it's going wrong tonight."

"This is one of those don't-call-the-cops deals?"

"More like an only-call-a-certain-cop deal."

"Ah." She shifted, taking in the motivationa posters. "In the gym? Who does that?"

"Angry Russians who own meathead gyms." H gave her a hand. "There's a jammer. No cell servic They can throw this place on lockdown in a heartbeat."

"I know." She reached to the top of the desk for he pointless cell. "Nothing."

"Stay." Bishop scooted to the desk, snagging brochure and a permanent marker. "Get to your car Call this number. Can you do that? *Only that?*"

"Jeez. It's like you know me already."

"I'll get Lexi safe, first priority. Russians, second Now, move."

Sugar smiled. "Total Titan material." She raised he fist, and he bumped it with his.

"Jared Westin's pregnant damn wife. In wha world...?" He covered her as she headed for the from door. As soon as she hit the parking lot, Sugar ran as fast as she could, hitting Refresh every other stride until she had a cell signal.

Finally, the cell rang. "Speak fast. I'm getting on a plane in an hour."

"Well, you better not do that," she said. "You've got a problem."

"Who is this?" All the humor left the man's voice.

"Your boy gave me this number. He's in trouble. My girl's in trouble. You have a pack of angry Russians causing it."

"Motherfucker."

"Probably that too." Sugar opened the door to her Range Rover and pulled herself into the driver's seat, taking more than a moment to focus on not grunting and groaning into the phone. That stomach of hers was getting very large.

"Where's Bishop?" the man asked.

"Crawling the rafters? Slinking behind treadmills? He said something about being Superman. So clearly, he thinks highly of himself, but still, he's smart enough to know he needs backup."

"Who are you again?"

"His pregnant partner in crime."

"Hang on—" A minute later he was on the phone again. "I knew better to plan a damn honeymoon until every last one of them was behind bars. Text me your location. Stay out of sight. Be there in twenty."

Sugar followed directions, texted as told, then called her husband.

Jared answered on the first ring. "Hey, Baby Cakes."

"Heya."

"See the maybe-new guy?"

"In passing."

"So?" Jared said.

"Hire his ass. You want that dude on your payroll."

He chuckled. "Ten-four."

"Alright, call you later."

"Hey, Sugar?"

"Yeah?"

"Whatever your sweet ass isn't telling me, I want a full report later, baby. Stay safe, be smart."

She couldn't hide the grin. He knew her too well. "Absolutely. Later."

CHAPTER 5

JARED LEANED BACK IN HIS office chair, tapping his fingers together, knowing full well that Sugar was beyond qualified to get herself out of whatever mess she'd found herself in. Otherwise, she would have flagged for help.

However, there was something in her voice…

He cracked his knuckles. Whatever she didn't want him involved in would likely be entertaining, fun, or dangerous. All of which he wanted in on. No, she wouldn't do danger while pregnant. She wasn't stupid. But she would do an adrenaline rush.

He picked up the desk phone and punched Parker's office extension. "Call Lexi. See what they're up to."

"I'm not getting into the middle of it with you two." Parker typed in the background. "If Sugar's giving you a headache, that's on you."

"Asshole."

"Boss Man."

"Pull up their phones," Jared said.

The tone of voice did the job, because Parke stopped with the bullshit and didn't have a comeback "Alright. So…" He hummed. "Lex's phone isn' picking up on screen, and Sugar's is stationary."

"Stationary, where?"

"Strip mall, Maryland, forty-five minutes from here."

"Comb the area. Give me everything you have within a half mile that looks a hair close to sketchy."

"Are the girls okay?" Parker's keyboard click-clacked in the background.

Jared looked at down at Thelma. Her instincts were spot-on, and the bulldog groaned and rolled over.

"What's going down in that neighborhood?" Jared asked.

"Here's something—a strip of real estate owned by an LLC that the FBI has flagged as belonging to the Russians." Parker's keyboard noises continued. "State PD has the area as a high point of interest. Task-force type crap."

"*Shit…*"

"Shit," Parker repeated.

"Run Bishop O'Kane's file again. See if there's anything we have about him working on a job related to the Russians."

"There's not, but let me look." The typing stopped,

nd Jared wanted to know everything. "Man, you know ur boy, Bishop—"

"He's not ours yet."

Parker hummed. "Let's see if there's a connection) Bishop and anyone working the Russians right ow."

"So?"

"Gonna need a second, Boss Man."

"Work faster."

"Is Lex in trouble?" Parker's voice dropped.

"I don't know what we're dealing with. Why don't ou tell me already?"

"Alright. Shit." Parker worked in silence, and time icked by too slowly. "Bishop O'Kane has one onnection, who…let's see. There's two solid points of onnection but the same circle of friends. He has a uddy on the Russian task force."

Jared grumbled. "Damn it to hell."

Parker agreed. "You going to tell Sugar?"

"I think she already knows."

"Right. And Lexi's phone's off—why?"

Jared rubbed his chin. "That, I can't tell you."

"Hang tight. I have some phone numbers for 3ishop." A minute ticked by. "Yeah, they're not howing up anywhere."

"Call Sugar." Jared leaned back in his chair. "Patch er in." A second later, the ringing phone made Jared's ;ut churn. With each ring, he should have felt better.

Lexi's phone would go straight to voicemail. Sugar'
was still on.

"I said I'd call back," she snipped as she answered.

Relief and irritation flooded him. "Baby Cakes."

"What?"

Jared put the phone on speaker and then rested hi
elbows on the desk and steepled his fingers. "Parker'
on the phone."

"Hi, Parker. Glad it's a party," Sugar said. "I'v
found myself an off-duty copper named Steve Zellers i
we're talking about a guest list to the phone-call party."

"Steve Zellers, lead on the Russian task force?"
Parker asked. "Who's set to go wheels up on hi
honeymoon in about ten minutes?"

"Man, you people know everything. Yeah. That'
me," a man said, grumbling. "The Russians do nothing
for months. I take a couple days off, get married, an
we've got angst in the ranks of the Gornovsky clan."

"What kind of angst?" Parker's voice dropped low
"Lexi in there, Sugar?"

"Bishop's got her in mind. He's on his way to ge
her out."

Jared knew that was Sugar's most comforting voice
but he also knew Parker—a control freak to the max
Any man on their teams would go apeshit in tha
situation, wanting to grab his woman and bring he
home. But Parker ran risk analysis. Jared knew that a
that moment, Parker's brain, whether deliberately o

not, was running the mortality percentages, determining if Lexi would be a casualty or would walk away unharmed. Everything in Parker's mind was a math problem of some sort—all jobs came down to risk, adversity, avoidance, and acceptance.

"Parker," Jared said. "Bishop's good. Top-notch. You told me that yourself."

"Nobody's better," Zellers added. "So long as we keep this contained, I'll be on my way to Tahiti by the end of the day."

CHAPTER 6

BISHOP SLIPPED BACK INTO THE large storage room and identified Lexi immediately. There were two men who fit the demographic of the gym's clientele. They were amped up and stupid enough to try something. Both had barbells in hand as though they would use the metal handles as weapons when the Russians came back into the locked room.

Exercise equipment versus Russian-made automatic weapons. *Genius.* Lexi, however, sat on a pile of old mats in the corner. She didn't interact with the men. She simply stared at her phone.

Bishop emerged from the corner where he'd been watching. The two other men likely hadn't noticed he was there to begin with, but she would have noticed he was missing.

"Hey."

Her gaze warily bounced to his. "Hey."

"I'm back."

"I don't know if that was smart or stupid."

He popped a squat next to her. "I met Sugar."

"Ah, smart." Her defenses went down. "So you know about us."

Bishop let a smile break. "In a manner of speaking."

"Sugar does this kind of thing. I *do not*."

He nodded. "What's your specialty?"

"I'm a hacker."

Her nerves looked to be getting the better of her. Fidgeting and tying herself into a little ball said loud and clear that she wasn't a woman who had a ton of field experience. The last thing that he wanted was for her to be terrified—although the situation was unnerving. "Pretty cool."

Lexi nodded. "Does me no good now, though."

"You have me. Pretty sure Sugar's told my partner by now we need a hand. We'll be good soon."

"Jared will have figured it out." Lexi fidgeted with her phone. "And he'll rain hell."

"Titan does what Titan does."

Lexi gave a weak smile. "You'll like it there."

Bishop nodded. "It's a job. I'd like to get it." *But that might be a lost cause now.* "Maybe one day. Maybe not."

"Why?"

He rolled his lips into his mouth. "I tied Sugar to a chair."

Lexi's jaw dropped, and she turned to him. Finally, the nerves and fear were gone, and something—amusement?—changed her demeanor. "Get the hell out of town."

He covered his face, rubbing his chin. "Yeah, well, you never know who's an enemy."

"Total Titan material." Lexi's eyes danced with humor. "Circumstances aside, I would have died to see that. Just so you know."

He chortled quietly. "Yeah, I get the impression that might not be par for the course for her. She was actually giving me tips as I disarmed her."

"Total Sugar."

"She'd armed herself with paper clips and scissors. Not sure what she was going to do with them, but I have a feeling she could've done damage."

"No doubt." Lexi took a deep breath. "Who are the guys who brought us back here?"

"Russians. It sounds like they're upset that someone on their team is missing."

"That's not good."

He nodded. "So this is the deal. We hang tight. If I see an opportunity to get you out of here, I'm taking it. Otherwise, we sit pretty until my guy does something."

"And what if he doesn't?"

"Then I suspect Titan will blow the roof off the joint." He made a playful *boom* noise, trying to prepare her, hoping not to scare her. "If that's the case, I'll just jump on you and try not to smash you. Deal?"

Her smile flickered and wavered. "Deal."

They bumped fists. With every person he met at Titan, Bishop wanted the job more.

CHAPTER 7

THE METAL DOOR SWUNG OPEN, and Russian voices arrived before Lexi could see the men. "Up. On your feet."

The two men with weight bars in their hands swung stupidly into action, just as Bishop had said they would do. And as predicted, the Russians quickly disarmed them. One moron nursed a head wound, and the other cried in the corner. Very manly.

Blood didn't normally bother her. However, she hated that they made no attempt to clean up. Red drips ran down their faces. Her stomach churned, but she followed directions, standing next to Bishop.

Another man came in the room, speaking what had to be Russian, and they ordered the bleeders to their feet.

"What are they saying?" she asked Bishop as soon as they had enough privacy.

"I'm not sure." His gaze darted. "I think we're on the move."

"To another room?"

"Not likely."

"Why?"

He gave an intense, fact-finding look at the room. "Don't know."

"Why are they keeping us?"

"*That* I really don't know. Doesn't make sense."

"Bishop..." Her stomach did more than churn. It was a churn-slash-ready-to-puke combo. "What, are they going to kill us?"

He didn't answer, his eyes intent on figuring out what was going on. That didn't bode well.

With a slight shake of his head, he relieved some tension. "If they were going to kill people, they would have offed Tweedledum and Tweedledee over there."

Right. No need to just knock the guys around when a simple bullet would do.

"They're typically not in the wet-works business," Bishop continued. "They move drugs, chemicals, things of that nature. Sometimes weapons. They like to make a profit. Hiding bodies and creating a list of warrantable crimes in the US is not on their priority list."

"So they won't?"

"Never say never, but let's just plan for the best, prepare for the worst, et cetera."

Et cetera. "Super comforting."

"I'll lie to you next time." His eyes continued to art around the storage room.

"Thank you," she whispered and prayed Bishop vould keep his promise.

CHAPTER 8

TITAN HAD EYES IN THE sky—surveillance hacked through as many systems as Sugar was sure Parker could manage on short notice. They didn't have much to go on with the jammer in place, though. Sugar and Zellers watched all exit points from their covert position in the neighboring parking lot, waiting for the next move. The slow passage of time made her sick. She couldn't imagine where Parker's head was at.

"What in Sam hell do you think is going on there?" Zellers tapped on the steering wheel.

The back door of the gym popped open, and two hulking guys hustled to large, dark SUVs. A quick second later, they moved the vehicles closer to the building, and the door opened again. Walking in a line, two men in gym gear plus Bishop and Lexi walked under the watchful eye of two other Russians and were funneled into the waiting vehicles. Bishop and Lexi stuck together, and the other men went into a differeı car.

Another Russian walked to a third vehicle, and th cars made their own little caravan as they pulled out o the parking lot.

Sugar rubbed her protruding belly. "They're playin line leader, and everyone wants to go home?"

"Smart-ass." The cop grimaced. "There goes Tahiti."

"Parker, what're you hearing?" Jared asked through the encrypted channel on Sugar's speakerphone on the center console.

"Nothing on the wires."

"Zellers?" her husband snapped. "Where are they going?"

"Jeez. Let me just snap up my mob-mind-reader and check."

"Asshole. Clearly you're not in control of the situation. Task force is done. Titan is in."

"Look," Zellers grumbled. "Titan means red tape. You guys cause your share of problems."

"Like not reporting a hostage situation to your superiors?" Parker asked, sounding none too thrilled with the direction the conversation was taking.

"Alright," Sugar interrupted. "Clearly, we're not all playing nicely—"

"Hang on, I'm hearing something." Parker paused. "What do you know about…?"

"What?" Jared snapped.

"Give me a second. I'm trying to figure out what the hell they're talking about."

"Damn it, Parker."

"My wife's in that car," Parker said. "Chill a second, Boss Man."

Jared shut his trap. *Score one for Parker.* Sugar waited to see what Parker would find. He worked fine under pressure or when Jared was yacking down his neck. He could handle this situation with Lexi, but still, he worked better when no one screwed with him.

"Zellers…" Parker's unsteady voice didn't bode well for whatever he had figured out. "What do you know about a chemical called Chepetsk?"

Zellers's head dropped. "Goddamn it."

"What?" Sugar asked.

He rubbed his temples. "If that's what this is about, we actually do have a problem, and I have to call my new wife and beg for forgiveness. I'm not going anywhere today."

"*What* is it?" Jared jumped in.

"Chepetsk isn't a chemical. It's a place. A city. Kirovo-Chepetsk."

"Yeah. That." Parker agreed. "What's the deal?"

"There's a chemical plant there. It's on a couple of converging rivers. They make fertilizers. The waste hit the water stream, and the company pays off whoever they need to pay off to make the stuff illegal and profitable. The stuff is poison; the town folk drink it."

"So why are they in Maryland fighting over it?" Jared asked.

"Searching everything I can find now," Parker said. "Other than the obvious, fertilizer can be used to make explosives. But why we're talking about it is another question."

"They hired a scientist from these parts, basically, and brought him in from wherever—Iowa, Nebraska, I don't know—against his will. Who knows the whole story—whether the guy thought he signed on for a good job and it turned bad, or a bad job and he got in over his head—but the Feds caught wind."

"Caught wind how and when?" Jared asked.

Zellers blew out and stretched in the driver's seat, putting the car in drive and merging into traffic as they followed the caravan from a good-enough distance. "Not sure, exactly. We have a bit of a communication issue."

"Shocking," Jared said.

Zellers ignored him. "From what I've heard, the Feds grabbed him, got what they needed from him. So now he's gone, and to the Gornovsky folks, the guy is missing, and they're turning on each other."

"*Missing*, as in witness protection? *Or missing*, as in the scientist dude is bled out somewhere for snitching?"

Zellers shrugged. "Missing. What does it matter?"

Jared growled. "They're fighting over this guy, and ou people lost him? He could be in Russia."

"Not my people."

"Freaking bureaucracy," Jared snapped. "Where is e? Is he out of the country? With a Russian faction?"

"Not likely. He's not Russian—just, ya know, does ell with the Russians."

"Parker," Jared said, "find everything you can about iis guy, the greedy scientist—what's his name?"

"Render Rossi," Zellers said.

"On it," Parker said.

"That's definitely not a Russian name." Jared's nuckles crackled over the airwaves.

Zellers turned to Sugar. "What's he going to do? ind the guy? End the turf war himself?"

She smirked. "Probably." *Jackass.* "Whatever he oes, Lexi will come home safe, and you'll likely get ome kind of task-force medallion of accomplishment. o shut up, copper, and let my husband save your job."

"Damn, you're a handful."

They kept their eyes on the Suburbans ahead. Bishop was with Lexi, and that set Sugar's mind omewhat at ease. If and when it was advantageous, he ould likely overpower the mobsters. Though a move ike that would be dangerous. But her gut said he was a mart kid and would wait to make his move.

"*Holy shit...*" It wasn't often that Jared sounded qual parts in awe and shocked.

Sugar dropped her gaze to the phone as though she could see what had Jared mumbling in surprise. "What?"

"This greedy scientist?" The words came out slowly, as though he were piecing together a plan he was still unsure about.

"Yeah?" Sugar said.

"He looks a hell of a lot like Parker. Throw a pair of glasses on Parker, hide the fact that he has an extra thirty pounds of muscle, and I'd say you have a chemical-making friend of the Russians."

"I don't look like that guy," Parker said.

"Text me a picture," Sugar requested, and a hot second later, lo and behold, yeah, the guy looked a hell of a lot like Parker *but with glasses*.

"How well do they know the scientist?" Jared asked.

Zellers shrugged. "The Gornovsky players don't get into the lab much. I'd say they're more business-type guys. If they've met, it's been in passing. Maybe seen him across the room. They don't deal with the hired help, if you know what I mean. Right now, their interests only lie in Rossi because he's their money maker and is MIA."

"It'd be risky…" Jared said.

Zellers's face tightened. "Eh…what's he talking about?"

"It'll work." Sugar could picture Jared popping his

nuckles, making notes, and writing the plans, not aring whether Zellers gave a thumbs-up or not.

"Do they communicate in Russian?" Parker asked.

Zellers looked from the phone to Sugar, back to the phone. "Are you guys serious?"

"Get Nicola in your earpiece," Jared said. "She can translate anything you need to know. And start learning everything else about the Gornovsky crew."

The plan made perfect sense to Sugar. Hesitation scored Zellers's face. His eyebrows arched painfully high, but before his mouth could protest, Parker broke in. "We've pulled off crazier shit. I'll do whatever needs to be done to get Lex home."

Just another reason why Sugar loved Boy Genius. He fuckin' rocked. "Get the man a pair of glasses."

CHAPTER 9

WITHIN FIFTEEN MINUTES, PARKER KNEW everything he needed to know about Render Rossi. Another twenty minutes, and he was fluent in Gornovsky business relations. Parker could broker a deal long enough for Titan and the Russian task force to show up, bust them all, save Lexi, and call the day a win.

Jared and Zellers had the details worked out for the why and how, and honestly, Parker had listened. But it didn't matter. His woman was in danger, and even though they played it down and promised that Bishop had hands on her and Sugar had eyes on her, Parker still knew that she wasn't safe.

His phone buzzed with a text message from Jared.

Jared: *You good to go in 15 min?*
Parker: *Yes*
Jared: *Winters and Rocco are ready and waiting*

All of that he knew. Brock's Delta team waited nearby. Winters could be counted on to blow the side off a building when need be, and Rocco could drive the hell out of a getaway vehicle if they needed to get Lexi out of there faster than Parker could get his arms around her. Backup plans upon backup plans.

Jared: *Russians got the news, bait's taken.*
Render Rossi will be at the Belvoir
Hotel.
Parker: *Good. Let's get Lexi safe.*

Titan had agreed to work hand in hand with the task force. Lexi would come home under Titan's command. The task force needed a live wire to pick up a transaction between the Russians, and then they could scoop up several arrests. Easy. They'd clean the streets of mobsters, and Parker would walk out with Lexi. No gunfire. No burning buildings.

Once the deal was done, assuming all went well, there would be no need for Winters, Rocco, and Delta team—those Delta guys were more trigger-happy than he'd seen on a team in a long time.

Parker inhaled deeply. *Yeah. Okay. Alright.* Lexi in this situation made him nervous. Hell, standing in this part of Titan HQ was unfamiliar to him. He looked around at the room he'd been in only a few times.

Mirrors. Wardrobes. Drawers. It was an entire room dedicated to subterfuge.

"What am I doing in here?" he mumbled. Computers and electronics, he knew. This stuff? Parker rubbed his face. Not a clue.

Beth, Roman's wife and a CIA consultant, was on the fast track to Titan HQ to help him perfect his look.

Give him anything he could hack, and he was good to go. A database that was unbreakable, or a security system that no one could get through? Yeah, he was in there. He'd gone undercover more times than he could count.

Yet this was different. His world was on the line.

So far, he'd donned a pair of khaki pants, a button down, and a jacket. Not too shabby looking, thank you very much. His black hair worked, and he popped in dark-colored contact lenses, making his eyes burn. "These things suck."

Blinking to stave off the blinding pinch, he tried to get the thing on the right part of his eyeball just as Beth walked in.

"More contact solution."

"Hey, yeah. Shit. Okay." He put another squirt in, gave a few more blinks, and it slipped into place. She was right. "Thanks."

"Alright, let's see what we're working with here." Her gaze started at his eyes, slowly made its way to his shoes, then went back up. "Holy shit, Parker. You made the greedy mad scientist freakin' hot."

He blushed and grumbled, futzing with his shirt. "Not the goal, Beth."

"But still, you nailed it."

"What now?" He turned for the mirror. Yeah, he looked like Render Rossi. But something was off, and he had no aesthetic expertise to know what was missing.

"Sit down," Beth ordered. "Like you didn't know you had good looks." She grabbed a tube of hair gel, forced him into a chair, and proceeded to muss his hair.

"This isn't what the picture looked like, Beth." He watched as she expertly made a disaster out of his hair, yet it looked fine.

"If you show up looking exactly like the picture we have on file, and you're a hair off, it's a dead giveaway that you're a freaking stand-in for the real deal." She mussed his hair all over again and took a step back to admire her work. "*But* if you're sporting a new look, it's fine." She stepped to him again, moved *one* piece of hair, and stepped back, stared, then wiped her hands on a towel. "Complete. Done. I'm a hair guru."

"And modest about it too." But she was right. Beth could do hair. "Roman's hair could look a lot better if this is the kind of power you possess."

She laughed, still staring at her work. "You know what, professor?"

"Hmm?" He rolled his eyes.

"I'd do you." She folded her arms across her chest. In a purely professional, just-kidding manner."

He rolled his eyes, again, but harder. "Focus."

"I am. Jeez. No one ever questions the hot guy. Trust me. That's a tip from a CIA pro." She turned for her purse and pulled out a glasses case. "Talk about nerd porn." Beth snapped the case open and pulled out the glasses. "Put them on now. I have to see."

He gave her the evil eye. "Only if you behave."

"Promise." She made a cross over her heart.

Parker unfolded the glasses and watched her as he put them on. "*Behave, Beth.*"

"Oh. My. Effin. God." She basked in her creation and turned him toward a mirror. "You are seriously utter nerd-boy perfection."

"Beth…"

"People do man-candy model shoots that don't look nearly a tenth as orgasm-worthy as you right now."

He glared. "Would you take this seriously?"

"I am serious as a heart attack. If you don't look the part, no one's buying shit. And brother, *you look the part.*"

He turned back to the mirror. "Yeah. Works, huh?"

"Totally. Plus, you'll get laid tonight."

He shook his head, feeling the tips of his ears burn. Alright. Out. Let's go. Out the door."

But he turned and grabbed one more glance over his

shoulder at the mirror. Not that he wouldn't get laid anyway, but if Lexi had a serious reaction in *any* way like Beth's over-the-top joking reaction, rescue night would be…fun.

That was not at all what he needed to focus on. But for all Beth's screwing around, he had finally relaxed and knowing Beth, that had been the point of her antics. *Ding, ding, ding.* She did everything for a reason. "Thanks, Beth."

She twisted as she powered down Titan's hall, winking over her shoulder, knowing he'd figured out her grand plan. "Anytime."

Time to bring his woman home.

CHAPTER 10

THE AIR CONDITIONING BLASTED AS Jared drove to the Belvoir Hotel. Parker sat in the passenger seat, and the teams were already in place. They were two men on the way to where their worlds—their wives—were. Parker's was in a more precarious situation, but that didn't matter. A pregnant Sugar could get herself into trouble no matter what the situation.

Jared's tight throat tensed, and he popped a Tums. Even if Sugar swore up and down that the feeling she gave him was the remnant or the anticipation of orgasms, this time it really *was* indigestion.

Parker perched quietly in his seat, arms crossed, waiting for the moment he could charge across the parking lot and meet with the Russians. "Doing okay over there?"

"Yup."

The last few months—hell, the last few years—shit

had changed at Titan. The guys had grown up. Before they'd all been brothers in arms, fighting the good fight, tearing up the world, making it better, bleeding because shit went down, bruising and busting heads because why not? They'd grab some broads and head home to blow off steam after a job.

Times had changed.

He wanted his woman and his family. He had the big-ass house. He had the cars, the trucks, the guns, the money. Jared had it all. When Sugar and Asal had come into his life, all that hard-living shit had seemed so…pointless.

He'd bust his ass to keep it all, to keep them pampered.

"*You* okay?" Parker turned the question on him.

Jared rubbed his chest, readjusting the seat belt. "How long have you been with Titan?"

"Let's see…more than ten, less than twenty."

"Years," Jared mumbled.

"Yup."

"A lot of hell has gone down."

"A lot of jobs," Parker agreed. "Most of which have gone right, and this one will be fine. If that's what you're worried about."

"No." He chewed his lip, exiting off the interstate. "Just… Colby has kids. Everyone's pregnant. Having babies."

"Sugar's about to pop any day, right?"

"Next few weeks."

Parker chuckled. "Doc Tuska going to deliver your kick-ass little bundle of joy?"

He smiled, shaking his head, reminded that he'd come full circle. "Not his area of expertise."

Shifting in the passenger seat, Parker asked, "You guys were Rangers together?"

"We were." Jared nodded as he changed lanes. Tuska was their medic, the man on the team sent to offer what he could during the storm of combat. He'd also been in the hell of Africa when Jared was at that life-altering pinnacle in his life, when he'd stood there with Buck Baer, and when they'd gone down separate roads. Baer, Tuska, and Jared each saw warlords destroying their own people. The three of them crawled through mass graves and hid their faces as tears slipped down their cheeks.

But each man had reacted differently to seeing genocide. Baer internalized it and rotted. He started GSI to make money and wield power. Tuska could've gone the Doctors Without Borders way, wandering around the world, administering aid and holding hands, but decided to focus on private practice. Jared had a steady supply of *clients* for him over the years, and their partnership continued. But in reality, Tuska had used his field experience and medical genius to raise money and awareness for people and places ignored by politicians.

Jared ran his hand over his cheek. His reaction t witnessing genocide had been to start Titan. Baer wa greedy. Tuska worked for a greater good. Jared ha seen a way to do the things that needed doing, whethe or not his government—or any government—wanted t get their hands dirty.

It paid well enough that he could do jobs that didn' pay a dime. He could recruit and command the best an the brightest, expand at will, and ignore red tape.

And it provided for a safer world for his family "Funny how life prepares you for the next big thing."

"Sugar would kick your ass for anything resembling a comment about her as the next big thing." Parke snickered.

Jared slowed down on a two-lane road. He smiled "No shit."

"Right." He paused. "You ready?"

"Of course I'm ready. Dick." When the hell wasn' he ready for everything and anything?

More laughter. "Ass."

"Yup," Jared said. "Point being?"

"You're going to do a hell of a job with a newborn." The words hit him like a throat punch. Jared grunte his agreement. "Tell me something I don't know." Bu maybe that was his concern. Everyone listened to him He'd yanked Asal off a cliff, and she became hi daughter. He'd sparred with Sugar, and she became hi wife. His team listened to him yell and give orders

hey respected the fuck out him because he was good
t his job. He knew the right moves—the best tactical,
trategic way to win in almost any situation.

But a newborn baby? That little girl wouldn't be
orced to love him. There was no fighting and
ntagonizing the kid to endear her to him. He took care
f people the way he knew how: by *telling* them how
est to do things then making sure they listened to him.
Ie wasn't Boss Man for nothing.

Babies didn't listen. They called the shots. He was
ompletely and categorically out of his comfort zone.
Vhat was he going to do about that?

F **PARKER HAD WORKED ONE** job undercover for
`itan, he'd worked a hundred. He could broker with the
ad guys and shoot a target a hundred yards away with
is eyes closed. Whatever the situation was, Parker
enerally handled it with a certain amount of calm,
oolness, and collection. He knew with precision
ccuracy what the risks were and what triggers and
olutions would mitigate them.

That was his normal. Lexi in a room changed the
ame. Even though his risk analysis said this was a
elatively safe operation, he didn't like it.

Parker pulled at the starched collar and pushed his

glasses up his nose. Wearing them already felt lik second nature. The earpiece went live, and in Titan HC Cash Garrison manned his office.

"Alright, Parker. We've got eyes on your buildin and from your shirt. Give me a test."

Parker coughed.

"We've got sound streaming live."

Parker nodded and pushed into the front doors c the hotel. His two Russian points of contact waitec their eyes narrowed on him with a calibrated focus. H swallowed, praying to God that Beth's new hairstyl trick was worth its salt.

One man stood, then the other. Both were clearl armed, and he, the greedy scientist, was *not*. Not idea All Parker had was a computer bag. It had a knif tucked into the lining of the fabric, but a blade versus bullet? Even on a good day, the odds weren't great.

They approached, and Parker extended his hanc "Gentlemen."

They grumbled and groused in Russian. On nodded his head, and pleasantries were obviously of the table. They left the hotel lobby briskly and walke down the hotel hall.

"Where have you been?" the taller, blonder on asked.

"Working."

"For us. You work for us."

"I have a real job," Parker said.

"You haven't been there."

"They send me to conferences, site visits." His gaze swept the room numbers, keeping his team visually in the know about where he was. "Minnesota. Iowa. I tested fertilizer in Iowa. Poor cell services; I know I've been hard to connect with lately."

The other Russian grumbled as they stopped. Parker took note of the room number as the two men opened the door. He hoped to see Lexi but also knew that they wouldn't walk him into the same place they were holding—

Well. So he was wrong, and statistically that was an anomaly, so rare an occurrence his palms tickled with sweat. How had he been wrong when it came to Lex?

The hotel room was a suite. Several men and Lexi sat, not looking completely uncomfortable, while the Russians and their weapons hovered nearby. Some reality trash TV was playing that he vaguely remembered Rocco loved the hell out of. Lexi looked up and...*please*...she didn't say a word.

Of course she wouldn't.

Their entourage proceeded to the kitchenette, and then one other joined their group, pulling chairs out at a small table. Parker's blood pressure climbed. If he was wrong about her in the room, what else would he be wrong about?

"Sit." The man's weathered face showed years of

war and tyranny. Speaking in a thick accent, he sounded unamused that Rossi had gone missing.

"Sure thing." Parker swallowed away his unease and pulled out the only chair left, setting the bag on the table after he made sure that his camera scanned all faces in the room. "So about my disappearance. I know it's not great business etiquette. I want to apologize."

A powerful hand slapped the table, and for a second, the entire rickety piece of hotel furniture almost gave way. "You owe us—"

"It's here." He patted his computer bag. "But what's with the peanut gallery?"

"That's your incentive."

"For?" Parker raised his eyebrow and ignored the trepidation thumping in his blood. "I'm good for the work. You know that."

"You went missing. *We do not know that.*"

He dropped his eyebrow and shrugged. "Point taken." He opened his computer. "We have three things that we last left off with."

"Get to the only one I care about," the hand slapper said.

"Alright." Parker had read Rossi's file and knew to expect this man as the head honcho. He was clearly the highest-ranking Gornovsky man in the room. In the city of Kirovo-Chepetsk, the man was a corrupt, dictator-like ruler—the bad-seed kind who didn't mind poisoning the rivers with the runoff from his chemical

ompanies and making a nice profit from weaponizing
ertilizer.

"You disappear—my trust in you has all but
anished. Tell me what I want to know."

Parker's spine stiffened, and he leaned forward,
esting his elbows on either side of his laptop. "Then
ay me."

The Gornovskys stared as though the greedy scientist
ad broken Russian business etiquette, and maybe he
ad. But it was too late to be concerned about that.

"You want the formula. I want my bank transfer."
arker closed his laptop. "If you pay, I'll tell you
vhatever you want, create whatever you need. *You
now this*. But if you don't authorize the transfer now,
'll disappear. Again."

A man who Parker decided was number two in the
ecking order cleared his throat and nodded to the
rowd on the couch, one of whom got up and placed
wo Makarov semiautomatic pistols on the table. The
hreat had been made.

They stared. He stared. Parker's blood thumped,
ulse racing. Sweat trickled down the back of his neck.
Vrong once before, he needed to read this situation
ight.

He narrowed his gaze on the leader. Everything
arker needed to know was there as he tried to read his
nind, to see the gray area in the black-and-white world
hat the guy lived in.

The Russian's eyes narrowed. His jaw flexed Anger? Impatience? Or was it a hollow threat?

The man was greedy. What Parker offered stood to make millions, and the time lost to finding another Rossi...if Render had been that easy to replace, they would have done it already.

"I work for you." Parker pointed at the lead, Gornovsky, playing to his ego. "Not *him* or the rest of your underlings."

There was a shift of testosterone, an uncomfortable challenge made. But Parker was right, and the man let out a sputtering of Russian without taking his eyes off Parker. There was no doubt what the words had been. They weren't *Kill the woman* or *Shed blood*. They were clear and simple: *Pay the man.*

Parker and Gornovsky didn't turn but remained eyeball to eyeball. Another man pushed out of his chair. Parker forced his hands to steady, needing to remain stoic and not check for a gun pressed to Lexi's temple. His heart slammed in his chest, and for a moment, he prayed that his calculated risk was right and that Lexi wouldn't be a casualty and Render Rossi's bank account was about to be filled with an illegal Russian payment.

"Pay the man."

The Russian barked into the phone, and Parker hid his sigh of relief.

Shaky seconds later, a slip of paper was handed to

Gornovsky, and only then did the man look away from Parker. He read it and nodded, sliding it across the table. "Your bank transfer."

Parker nodded, opening his laptop again. "And now for your—"

The hotel room windows rattled as the door burst wide. The familiar-enough sound of a raid stabbed him with shock as booted men wielding high-powered weapons swarmed.

"Police! Everybody down on the ground."

The Russian task force engulfed the space. Shouts repeated, voices escalating. "Faces on the ground. Get down. Weapons down. Police."

The Russians complied but with menace and threats that needed no words.

The civilians shouted their innocence and begged for help.

Bishop covered Lexi, and Parker took a deep, thankful breath, slowly unfolding himself from the chair, keeping his cover as Render Rossi and dropping to the floor alongside his cursing Russian counterparts.

They had what they needed for Gornovsky arrests, and his woman was safe. Job well done.

Chapter 11

Lexi would have been lying to herself if she said neither adrenaline nor worry had affected her thinking the whole day. But those feelings had gone. What still had her buzzing?

Parker—in those glasses. She wasn't one for fetishes. That wasn't even her thing. But those were *hot*.

And they were coming home. He could lose the khaki pants. Or maybe not. The button-down geeky-professor look did something for her too. It was different. As if he were another guy. His hair accentuated his bone structure, and his eyes were dark. It was fun. Like playing dress up.

She could feel her heart pounding in her chest. All she had to do was wait for him to come find her once this was over and—God, could these cops who had a million questions for her tell that she was hot and bothered—*because of a pair of glasses*?

The hotel room door opened, and there Parker stood, eyes searching the room. They landed on her. "Are you done with Lexi Black?"

She shivered at the way he said her name and how he owned her with an unwavering stare.

"Absolutely." Bishop strode forward to Parker, and they made introductions and small talk. Parker kept her in his line of sight until Bishop nodded good-bye, then he headed her way.

"Nice meeting you, Lex. For someone who says she doesn't do field ops, you were a pro."

A proud blush hit her cheeks. "Thanks, Bishop."

"Ready?" Parker asked. The tenor of his voice screamed that he wanted his hands on her as much as she wanted to get hers on him. It was less a question and more *Hurry the hell up*.

"Yup."

With a quick handhold, Parker moved her into the empty hall and had her pressed against the wall. "Lexi, damn it. All I wanted was you safe."

"Hey." She kissed his neck, nuzzling against him, and hugged his neck until he lifted her off the ground.

"You have no idea the thoughts that went through my mind." He squeezed her tight, and still she hung on.

"Same."

He put her down. "You in workout clothes? It's a good look for you."

Lexi raised her eyebrow. "You in glasses, crazy hot…where'd they go?"

"I forgot about these things." His hand went for his suit coat. With a quick move, he put them on and struck a pose. "Beth says they might get me laid."

Lexi laughed, and as Parker went to take them off, she jumped at his hand. "Don't you dare take those off."

With an amused smile, he shook his head, walking to the elevators. He pressed the button and pulled her against him. "All right. Fun is fun."

"I'm not kidding. Crazy hot. They might've been the only thing to get me through the last couple hours of questioning."

"Stop it." His eyes danced, and Lexi could've sworn he blushed slightly.

"Not a chance." The elevator dinged. "I saw you in your glasses and fantasized about my husband. It made hours feel like minutes."

His smile could have made her clothes melt away as he held the elevator door for her. "Then let's get home. We have to make a pit stop on the second floor. I need to grab my wallet and keys to a car."

She went onto her tiptoes and whispered in his ear. "As long as you don't take off those glasses."

He grabbed her ass. "Dirty girl."

"You like it."

Parker slid a key card into a hotel room. Jared and

Sugar were two steps from walking out as Parker and Lexi headed in.

"Looking good, Boy Genius." Sugar rested a hand on her stomach and let Jared pull her into the hall with the other.

"Sugar's exhausted. We're out," Boss Man said. "See you mañana?"

"You got it."

Lexi pushed her way into the hotel room as Parker continued to chat with Jared, dead set on collecting Parker's bag so they could go home as well.

But... Parker came back into the room, gathering his wallet and a set of keys. "Ready, sexy?"

"Anyone else have a key to this room?" Lexi leaned against the edge of the bed.

A smile curled on his cheeks as he turned to see her sitting with her best come-hither grin. "Nope."

"Just you and me. Those glasses, and—"

"Those yoga pants."

His hungry gaze went straight to her stomach, then below. If she'd been turned on before, then her husband had just lit a fire with a look. "You like?"

"It's a nice change of scenery." Parker strode forward.

"You're kind of like the professor right now."

His brows jumped predatorily. "I am?"

Lexi nodded. "Or maybe Mister CEO. The boss. Either way, super sexy." She ran her hands up his tomach, enjoying the feel of the starched shirt and his ock-hard body. Parker loosened his tie, and her hands ropped to his belt. "Can we play?"

"Undo the belt, Lexi."

Her stomach flipped into her throat. Anticipation he hadn't experienced before jumpstarted her already-aging arousal.

"Yes, sir." Slowly, Lexi unfastened his belt, letting he clasp clink, and then unzipped his pants.

His bulge made her come alive. Holding his hand ut, Parker backed into a chair and beckoned her orward. Lexi dropped to her knees, pulling his pants nd boxer briefs down as she went. Kneeling between is thighs, his massive erection in her hand, she eaned forward and licked from the base of his shaft the tip of his crown, lingering as Parker groaned. Iis sexy glasses and his tousled hair looked like her antasy come true, and she wanted to make sure he new it.

She kissed the top of his cock, slowly sucking, and vatched his eyes flutter shut, his jaw hinge open. Lexi iched down, swirling her tongue, groaning as his hickness filled her mouth and touched the back of her hroat.

"Shit, Lex." His hips bucked up as she wrapped her iouth around his head, still watching him.

What a gloriously beautiful man. He opened his yes, and she took him in, relaxing as best she could, loving how Parker filled her mouth, how her hand wrapped his shaft and worked him. Their eyes were connected even when hers watered.

Her tongue swirled the crown, and he spread his legs, trapped by the pants, letting his powerful thigh hug her. Lexi bobbed her head, worked her hands. His fingers threaded into her hair, and his hips found a rhythm with her mouth.

"Lex." Parker's voice went gravelly and sent shivers down her spine.

He was going to come, and she would make him love every second of it.

It was something about the damn glasses. Seriously. He even had a lazy, sated grin on his face that might've been one of her favorite looks ever.

Lexi rocked back off her knees and—

"Where do you think you're going?" he asked.

She blinked. "Um, I—"

"On the bed, Lex."

Her heart jumped. Wherever that sated, lazy grin had gone, it was g-o-n-e. Glasses or not, she knew that tone. That was the sound of Parker on the hunt. "Yes, sir."

He kicked off his shoes, followed by his pants. Parker untied his tie, letting it hang around his neck as he walked to where she sat on the bed. His nod was his unspoken command, and she unbuttoned his shirt.

Carefully, *reverently*, Lexi undid each little white button with shaking hands. His powerful physique stood godlike, and even if he wore clothes like this every day, she wasn't sure that she'd ever get used to it. She didn't want her normal Parker to change one bit, but this was luscious.

"Good," he said. "Very good."

Goose bumps sparked across her skin at the praise. "Thank you."

He snaked the tie off his neck in one quick pull, letting it drop to the ground. Lexi's eyes went wide as her core clenched. Parker shrugged off the button-down shirt and tore off the white undershirt until it was just him in glasses. "All for you, Lex."

She didn't want to wait for whatever Parker had in mind. She kicked off her shoes and tugged off her socks. There was too much fun to be had.

"Slow down, sweetheart. You're my package to unwrap."

"I can't. You're killing me. And you'll never get a sports bra off of me." Which was true. He was naked, and she wouldn't stay clothed—no way, no how.

"On the bed, baby."

"Thank you, Jesus."

He snickered, shaking his head, and crawled up to the headboard, pulling her with him. "I'm going to take the glasses off now."

She had her fill—his dark hair sprawled out on the

pillows, him reaching for the glasses. Who knew this was what it would take for her to go to heaven happy?

"Fuck it." He growled. "Look at me like that, and they're never coming off." He attacked her neck with kisses, teeth scraping, tongue lapping. His rock-hard erection pressed between her legs as his body burrowed between her thighs.

"God, Parker."

She used her hand to guide his cock, and he pressed against her slick slit. Holy…shit. He hadn't touched her all day. But she was more than turned on, and as he thrust inside her body, Lexi moaned and clawed his back, biting his shoulder, needing his cock to fill her.

He inched back and thrust again.

"Yes," she said, panting, her body adjusting to the invasion. "Again. Please."

He did. Deeper. Harder.

His chiseled body was a machine. He moved as though he knew her every breath, her every thought. Parker drove into her, gritting into her ear, cursing her for how good her pussy felt, how tight she felt, how hot she made him. Lexi arched into him, needing it all—the words, the rhythm, the intensity.

She wrapped her arms around his neck, and he buried his head against her hair. They were lost in each other, and as their orgasms slammed together, the only thing she could think or feel, the only thing she could emember as the stars exploded, was how Parker murmured in her ear how much he loved her.

Whispering and catching her breath, she felt her world begin and end with the man in her arms. "Love you too."

CHAPTER 12

ARED COULD COUNT ONLY A few times in his life he'd
een legitimately confused, and they included the last
ew hours. He popped a couple knuckles and tried to
nake sense of what he'd been watching and came up
lueless.

"Are you cleaning?" Jared eyed Sugar. For the third
ime, she rearranged a shelf in the kitchen pantry. It was
iotable since she didn't rearrange anything that didn't
iave ammo associated with it, and if she went into the
iantry, it generally involved eating. None of which was
iappening. So he was lost.

"Nope."

He continued to watch, wondering what the hell had
iappened to his wife. "Organizing, then?"

"No." She didn't turn around.

"What is it that you're doing?"

"Asal wants Jell-O."

That was not what she had been doing for the last few hours. "Do we have Jell-O?"

"I have no idea." Finally, she pivoted, exasperated. "But I'm not going to find the answer if you keep asking."

"Why don't I go and get some?" he said, thinking it might be a solution. Solutions were what he did best, but then again, this was not a well-defined problem. Jell-O was a symptom. Of what, he had no idea. Literally, there was no way Sugar had been looking for Jell-O for hours. Or had pregnancy made her lose her mind?

Sugar tugged a bright-red lip between her teeth. "And can you get some sour cream? That stuff is chronic on Cheez-Its."

"Check the fridge, Baby Cakes. You're fully stocked." He high-fived himself mentally.

Asal skipped into the room. "Check again, Dad. We're out."

Well, shit. How had he missed that search-and-destroy mission? "Okay. Back in ten." He grabbed his keys, kissed his girls, and headed for his garage, hollering over his shoulder, "Anything else?"

"Yeah," Sugar called. "Just one of everything." He heard them giggle and scoot out of the kitchen. "Come on, let's go play in the baby's room."

Apparently, in the last two days that meant folding and refolding *everything*, but whatever. Sugar liked it and Asal was excited for the baby to arrive.

As he punched the garage door open, he couldn't wipe the smile from his face, knowing that his badass wife, the one someone might mistake for a "biker bitch," was nothing more than a softie playing dolls with her kid and fussing over teeny baby outfits until they were *just* perfect.

And no one knew that despite Jared's growl and bite, those two girls and the one on her way could bat their little eyelashes, and he would bend God's will to get whatever they wanted. He was mush for them. And proud of it.

———————

THE BABY KICKED HER UTERUS again, and Sugar winced, trying not to curse in front of Asal. "Whoa, popsicles."

Popsicles. Not a creative curse word. It was probably an homage to her ever-rumbling stomach but was better than any number of things that could have come out of her mouth.

"I'm going to rock the baby like this." Asal had a doll in her arm and swayed back and forth.

"Awesome, honey." Sugar slowly made her way to the glider and eased herself into it. Asal propped herself on the footstool, fussing over the baby doll's clothes, then went to the changing table and pretended to change her doll with one of the newborn diapers.

A small contraction hit. As Braxton-Hicks contractions went, this one was light. They'd plagued her for the last few weeks, and while they were supposed to be the *practice* ones, they still sucked.

Buzz. Buzz.

Dang it. "Asal, hon. Can you grab my phone?" She was not standing up at the moment.

Dutifully scooping her baby doll into her arms, Asal grabbed Sugar's phone—the buzzing had stopped—and handed it to her. *Missed call: Jared.* She hit redial. If there was a shortage of sour cream, there was a good chance she was to blame.

"Hey."

"Hey, Baby Cakes. I hate to ask you this."

Sugar grumbled the same time another not-so-light contraction hit. "What's up?"

"I have a two-woman field team about to run an op for Delta. They have no gear, and Brock's over near GUNS. Can he swing by for a quick shopping spree?"

Brock was the commander of the Delta team. His wife, Sarah, was Sugar's business partner, and she ran her gun store and range while Sugar took it easy and prepared for maternity leave. "Yeah, yeah. Take what you need. Put it on your tab."

"Thanks."

"Want to tell me how a grocery run turned into an order to fully outfit"—she shifted to alleviate the iscomfort in her back—"two women I don't know?"

"All in a day's work."

"No juicy details, huh? I can't even live
icariously."

"Delta's rescuing a Honduran cartel wife."

"Ah." That probably had something to do with the
hitstorm Delta cleaned up a few weeks ago in Central
America. "Give me details later."

"You doing okay?" he asked.

"Of course. Just nosey." And uncomfortable and
rampy. Maybe contraction-y. Definitely. Another
ontraction started. She checked to see how long they'd
een on the phone. *Not that long.* "Did you get my
nacks?"

"Roger that. And Jell-O."

"Sweet. And you're on your way home?"

"Yeah. Why? Actually, I might stop—"

She took a short breath. "Hey, come home." Her
oice had dropped. Asal paused with her doll.

"Mom, you okay?"

"Yes, honey." Smiling at Asal, Sugar shifted again,
sing the glider—unsuccessfully—to try to ease the
iscomfort. "Jared."

"Already on my way."

CHAPTER 13

GRAVEL SPUN UNDER THE TIRES as Jared skidded onto the shoulder and then righted his SUV from the U-turn. Sugar wasn't one to panic. The woman would rather sit on a grenade and save a small town than let a modicum of sweat dampen her brow. That tinge of *get home quick* in her voice meant she was in pain, and there were very few times he'd heard his wife in a vulnerable state before. She'd be past the level of uncomfortable and likely timing a contraction or two before she'd let him in on what he already knew.

The woman was in labor.

He pressed the gas pedal, his heart pounding, and reached for his phone, dialing Mia Winters.

Mia answered on the first ring. "Please tell me Sugar's having a baby!"

He grumbled at Mia's over-the-moon excitement. His own excitement bordered on high blood pressure.

Everything was under control. He'd mapped all possibilities out. Everything had a plan. The plans had contingencies. He would be cool under pressure as always. But his wife was about to deliver his daughter.

He cleared his throat, cracking a knuckle for good measure. "She didn't say that."

"Why would she?" Mia rounded her kids up off the phone before coming back. "It's Sugar. On my way over."

"Could be nothing."

"Could be a baby!" Mia gushed.

When she said it like that, Jared's stomach jumped the way it had when he was that high-school freshman called out for varsity football. He had known it was coming, but when it did, it still shocked the hell out of him. But on the scale of exciting life events, varsity football versus a baby, the baby was magnified about a thousand times over. "Grab Winters."

"Colby's already wrangling Ace into a car seat."

"Good." Jared floored the gas when the light ahead turned yellow, ignoring what was certainly a heart palpitation in his throat. "Could be nothing."

"Then we have a pizza party with Asal, and Sugar can complain about heartburn."

"Right. See you soon." He hung up and tossed down the phone then thought better of it, pulling it closer in case Sugar called, as though those extra inches between him and the phone would make a difference. He cracked a knuckle and cleared his throat.

Sugar. Was. In. Labor.

Minutes later, Jared screeched into the driveway and jumped out. He left the garage door up because why waste time if he would haul ass out again? He burst inside, groceries in hand just in case he *was* blowing Sugar's tone of voice *way* out of proportion— although he knew he wasn't.

Asal's huge grin met him. "Mama's having the baby!"

Sugar hovered on the edge of the couch arm, not exactingly sitting, a forced smile on her face, gritting her teeth more than saying hello. "*Think so.*"

For one long-assed second, all of his plans went out of his head. They stayed locked in a look until Asal clapped. "Clara and Ace are here!"

Jared blew out a breath. "Backup. Alright. Good. They're here."

"Honey," Sugar said, taking a deep breath and turning her head to look at their daughter. "Colby and Mia and the kids are spending the night."

"*I know.*" Asal rushed to the front door to let them in. "You guys have only been over *the plans* a thousand times."

This was true. They were nothing if not well prepared. Though in the eyes of a ten-year-old, that was likely as boring and annoying as Asal had just made it sound.

The brood walked in. The kids went a million miles

an hour. Winters made a joke. Sugar threatened to kil him. Mia smacked her husband and went to Sugar to start timing the contractions. They were close but not close enough to head to the hospital. Jared turned on the oven, per Mia's instructions, *that little drill sergeant*, and took the bag of frozen pizza that she had brought over for the kids.

Clara and Asal ran through the living room with Ace in the back of a giant dump truck. "Don't dump your brother face-first on the floor," Winters yelled. He smiled and made his way into the kitchen.

Jared crossed his arms over his chest, watching their two families' lives unfold as Winters propped next to him against the counter.

"This is some crazy shit," Jared mumbled.

"Pretty damn awesome, huh?" Winters agreed.

Pride swelled in Jared's chest. Hell yeah, it was. He nodded at his guy, who went to grab a beer, and Jared went to his wife. Sugar had still opted to sit on the edge of the couch arm instead of the actual couch cushion, and she and Mia were lost in conversation about Delta team and the new Titan recruits.

He wrapped his arm around Sugar's shoulders, settling on the back of the couch, and she leaned her weight against him.

Ten years ago, if Jared had been offered a million dollars to predict the future of his household, there was no way he could've guessed correctly. Yeah, maybe he ould've nailed the fact that Winters would settle down. Maybe him too. But that his fortress of a house was…a ome? He took it all in: Happiness bounced off the walls as a pizza baked in the oven, and his impatient wife waited for a phone app to tell her it was time to ead to the hospital.

Could he have foreseen this? Never. He couldn't ave dreamed anything this great.

"Okay. Press that little damn button," Sugar rowled to Mia, who hit the start button on the phone. All four adults watched the timer. Actually, three— ared watched Sugar.

Ding. Ding.

Mia's eyes danced. "Baby time."

Chapter 14

THE OVERHEAD LIGHTS IN THE hospital's reception room glared. People milled around as though something momentous were not about to happen. Jared was on edge. He knew adrenaline. He knew anticipation. He wasn't at all prepared to sit and wait on paperwork, contractions, and a waiting area. Of all the places to have a waiting room, a hospital birth center seemed wrong. If he ran the joint, staff would be stationed here, directing traffic, giving orders to move at appropriate times. He'd have constant intelligence updates and live-streaming stats—where the doctor was, what the nurses were doing, when the rooms were ready.

Instead, he held a cheap plastic pen and a clipboard with information that had long ago been submitted to the hospital as Sugar had an intense moment. Her nails dug into his forearm. *A very intense moment.*

"Doing okay, Baby Cakes?" Jared adjusted Sugar'
grip.

"Never better." Her lips were a flat line, and if she
hadn't been ready to have a baby, he'd have assumed
she was a split second from a rage kill. He could see her
molars grinding behind her cheeks.

"Your fingernails are digging deep, babe. Though
I'd ask."

"Would you shut up a minute?" She dug back in.

Okay. Yeah, he would need stitches after Sugar had
the baby. That was fine. If that's what it took. He
flipped the form over. "Stupid paperwork. I thought we
did this ahead of time."

"We did."

"Why are we doing it again? Stay put." He removed
his wife's talons from the upper layer of his dermis and
walked back to the nurses' desk where they'd checked
in. "Hey, yeah. We already did this."

The nurse faked a smile. "That's day-o
paperwork."

"Yeah. It's done." He put it down.

"Both sides?"

No. "Everything you need is there." Honestly, he
didn't need to battle the lady, but as his chest puffed out
and he contained a megadose of alpha-hole, Jared made
a big show of signing the back page. He slid the
clipboard forward. "Done."

Sugar had wanted to go to *her* special hospital, no

where he basically had a concierge setup with Doc Tuska at *his* hospital. At this point, he would have paid to relocate her OB's practice. "*If* there's a problem, tell me about it. Otherwise, let's get this show on the road. *She's having a baby.*"

As if on cue, a man rolled up with a wheelchair. "Lilly Westin?"

Oh, brother. That would not go well. Before he could correct the poor soul with the wheelchair, he saw his wife's annoyed face.

"*Sugar.*" She pushed out of her chair. "That's me."

Jared growled at the nurse, the wheelchair guy—basically at the entire room. This was not going as smoothly as he had planned. That was fine. He lived for handling contingencies. However, beginner name-calling mistakes and day-of paperwork were not on his list of acceptable fuckups.

"Let's go," Jared snapped and led the way as if he knew where he was going. There was only one way to go. Down the hall. So off they went.

"How are we doing today?" the chipper man pushing Sugar's wheelchair asked.

Jared rolled his eyes and shifted Sugar's go-bag over his shoulder. "GTG, buddy. We're good to go. Get us to our room."

"I'm fine. Ready to do this already." Sugar took a deep breath. "Can you mark it down somewhere that I don't like *Lilly*? I thought that was already done."

"It *is* already done," Jared said.

"Well, her paperwork says—"

"Never mind." *Concentrate on the baby.* "We'll get you a name tag or something, Baby Cakes. Make sure it's clear."

"First baby, Dad?" The man slowed Sugar and swiped a badge to open an electronic door. The goofy grin on his moronic face easily said he didn't realize he treaded dangerously close to the end of his life.

"He's fine," Sugar answered for him. "Kid number two. We should cut the small talk—oohh." She groaned. "Probably best for everyone."

"Alright, here we go!" They wheeled into a room and parked Sugar, letting her breathe through her contraction. After a moment of logistics, Jared dropped her bag, and Sugar nestled into the bed as the wheelchair pusher was eyeballed out of the room.

Where was the streaming intel when Jared needed it? Where was the team that was supposed to hop into action?

A nurse came in, clearly warned that Sugar was *Sugar.* "Hi, *Sugar.*"

Jared breathed easier as she was hooked up to things that beeped and printed and dinged and began to spit out something that might be construed as helpful. All was back on course.

Moving from one side of the room to the next, he couldn't find a great vantage point that seemed ppropriate as the nurse dropped between Sugar's legs, naking his wife look far more uncomfortable than she needed to be. But more things had *progressed*. She was *dilated and effaced.*

He realized this was something he could never do, and couldn't imagine what strength Sugar needed. But, he was proud of her. And pacing, he worked his jaw, ignoring unusual nerves brought on by things that weren't in his control. Jared rolled his shoulders, wandering to the other side of the bed. He cracked a knuckle and worked his neck back and forth.

The machine's printout picked up pace, making *his* heart beat faster. "You doing okay?"

Her cheeks were flushed, her hair tied back, and Sugar had never looked more confident or beautiful as she dropped back onto a pillow. "Hell yeah."

God, he loved his woman.

"Sugar!" A man who looked more like a movie star than a real-life doctor swooped into the room.

"Hey, Doc." She popped her head up then dropped back again. "I'm having this baby."

"So I hear. And you must be Dad."

Jared looked at her, looked at him. "Who's this guy?"

"Dr. Archer. I'm delivering Baby Westin today."

How did he miss that Sugar's OB was a movie-star Doc? Not that he was the jealous type... "Why haven't we met before?"

"Are you serious?" Sugar snapped. "Did you go t- *every appointment?*"

"No." *With his wife's blessing*, he'd been working in hell zones around the damn world.

Dr. Archer laughed as if he knew her well. "Alright let's get our girl through this contraction and see how we're doing."

Right. He wanted to call the guy a dick, but the dude was right, and Jared was not in control of the moment. Of the three of them, he was the lowest man on the totem pole, and that was some shit.

He took a deep breath, trying to keep his shit together. As long as Sugar and the baby were healthy and safe, that was all that mattered. Doctor McDreamy could do his damn job and be on his merry way.

"Jared." Shaking him out of his thoughts, Sugar pulled him aside. The doctor agreed that she had more time to labor, and under the supervision of the nurses she was left to growl and grouse, to breathe and meditate with him as her focus.

Hours. It took them *hours*. He was exhausted and unable to imagine how she handled the stress on her body.

Dr. Archer walked into the room, smiling as though he were seriously on a TV show. "Alright, Sugar. It's time. You ready, honey?"

Jared's eyebrow ticked up, but he didn't say a word at *honey*. Instead, he held her hand, astonished at the

heer strength Sugar still had. The nurses said to push.
She pushed. He watched her eyes squeeze shut, tears
leaking out, veins popping at her temples and forehead,
her face turning shades of red that had him concerned.

"Breathe!"

"Deep breaths!"

She did, her eyes holding onto his and her hand not
letting go.

"I've got you, Baby Cakes. You can do this."

Sugar nodded.

Another contraction hit, and all the orders came
again. Sugar cried out, pushing and exerting herself as
hard as any man he'd ever seen. Actually, harder.

"Don't stop, honey."

"Keep going."

She cried. She pushed. She gave everything she had
to their daughter.

Their voices were loud, but he came close and
quiet. "You've got this, Sugar." Jared clung to her as
hard as she clung to him. "Push, Baby Cakes."

And then he heard it. She did too—the tiny sounds
of their baby.

Sugar fell back in exhaustion, tears dampening her
cheeks. Jared wrapped his arms around his wife, unable
to hold back. "God, Sugar. You did it. Baby. You did it."

When he looked up, there was their little girl. "Dad,
time to cut the cord."

And Jared's whole world was now complete.

CHAPTER 15

THE COLD AIR POURED INTO Titan HQ's war room. Rocco Savage, the second in command of all teams, Brock Gamble, who ran the Delta team, and Parker sat with Bishop O'Kane's folder in front of them and the man across the table.

Parker had to give the guy credit. He didn't flinch under scrutiny. They were an intimidating bunch, and this was an intimidating building. Bishop was there for the final interview of a much-sought-after job. Boss Man had already given his thumbs-up and was off the grid with Sugar. The final decision lay in their hands.

There was one question on the table: what would he have done differently about Sugar? This was where Bishop could lose the job. Everyone in the room knew it too.

Bishop's eyes crinkled, and he almost smiled but must have thought better of it. "I'd have figured her out earlier and let her stir in the jump ropes a minute longer."

Parker laughed. "Damn." He'd expected something more along the lines of sucking up about Boss Man's wife. But to let Sugar sit and wait? Parker laughed again.

Rocco and Brock did too.

"Careful," Rocco cautioned. "That woman could string you up and hide the body where no one would find it."

Bishop smiled. "Bet she could."

Brock remained silent and ran a hand over his face. "Works for me." He eyed Rocco, who gave Parker the go-ahead to excuse Bishop.

Parker stood and walked toward the door, the almost-new hire following in line, and he opened it and directed him to a small conference room nearby. "Good answer, bro."

"She's crazy, isn't she?" Bishop laughed.

"In the best of ways," Parker said.

They reconvened and agreed with Boss Man and Sugar's assessment. The dude was spot-on. They liked him and wanted to work with him. Brock nodded. Parker did too. Rocco slapped the table. "Alright, then."

They filed out, and Rocco stopped by the conference room where they'd left Bishop. "Welcome to Titan."

"**KNOCK-KNOCK. WE COME BEARING** gifts." Sugar's sister, Jenny, and her husband, Asher, walked into the hospital room, eyes trained on the sleeping newborn bundled in Sugar's arms.

Sugar grinned, exhausted and blissed out in a way that she couldn't explain. Having her sister walk in made it that much better. Family had always been a four-letter word, with the exception of her sister, until Jared had crashed into her life. He'd just left for the cafeteria to grab Asal and him lunch while she rested in a hospital bed. Asal was tucked on one side of her. "Heya."

Asal squirmed off the bed and jumped into Asher's outstretched arms.

"What's up, short stack?" Asher asked.

Her dark ponytail whipped Asher in the face as her excitement bubbled over, and she reached back for the bed. "I'm *awesome* at helping."

"Bet you are." He put her down, and they moved closer to Sugar. Jenny's tearing eyes went wide, and her pearly whites beamed.

"I know where the diapers are," Asal said. "I tell the nurses when they need to do things."

Sugar couldn't hide her amusement at the little boss lady in the making. Jenny and Asher had the same amused faces.

Asal turned for *her* diaper bag. "Plus, I have snacks. Do you want something?"

"I think we're good. How about you, Mama?" Jenny asked. "Need anything?"

"Jared went for lunch. He'll be back—"

As if on cue, he walked in with drinks in one hand and a to-go bag in another. "Hey, Jenny. Hey Mister Presidential Candidate." He chuckled quietly, so as not to wake the baby, and deposited the food on a table.

"Not yet, not yet." They shook hands. "If at all."

"Not what the papers are murmuring."

Jenny rolled her eyes. "Yeah, the press. Your favorite people. They always say the truth."

"Just keeping him on his toes," Jared said to Asher and Jenny repositioned at the corner of the bed. Asa dug into the takeout and began distributing the meals.

"She's beautiful." Jenny sighed, scooting closer to Sugar.

"I know," Sugar said.

"So?"

"So what?" Sugar asked.

"Come on. Don't make me beg."

"Oh." She laughed. "You want a name."

"Uh, yeah."

"Vi-vi!" Asal announced.

Jenny's questioning glance left the newborn and went to Sugar. "That's different."

"Hello?" The deep, low baritone of Jared's father announced his arrival before Sugar saw him.

"Hey, Pops." Jared greeted his dad, but Asal was

ead greeter, repeating her arm-launching manner of
aying hello.

"Grandpa." She wrapped her arms around his neck
ut quickly wiggled away. "Grandma!"

Violet Westin barely had a foot in the room before
Asal slingshot from one grandparent to the next. A
ound of hugs and kisses later, Asal dragged the older
woman over to the baby. "Grandma, this is *the other*
Violet."

"Oh," Jenny whispered.

Tingles ran down Sugar's spine as she glanced up
and watched her husband. The man could bark orders or
peak volumes with his scary silences. At this moment,
e crossed his thick arms over his impossibly broad
hest and stood stoically.

"Hi, Violet. Meet your namesake." Sugar gently
ilted her elbow up, adjusting the sleeping baby, then
elaxed her arm as Jared came up behind his mom.

"Mom." He kissed the top of her head.

Asal crawled onto Sugar's bed and snuggled in
lose. Jenny and Asher closed in too. This was
amily—everything Sugar had once thought a
ightmare. The emotion and exhaustion hit her for a
econd as voices began to talk around her, and she let
er eyelids slip. Maybe she tried to hide a tear.
Maybe she was choked with emotion. Maybe taking
t all in was too much. Or maybe this was just the
erfect moment, and never did Sugar think that

she'd be lucky enough to have a life like this.

She didn't realize how hard she'd fought for the fairy tale or that she'd been going after it to begin with. But what a journey it had been, and they were only getting started.

———————

JARED WATCHED THE TWO STRONGEST women he knew—his wife and his mother—and then his chest pulled with a tightness that could only be explained as a surge of pride. Asal and Violet would be just as strong as the two women holding them.

His dad was a man of few words, and as he stepped over to Jared, slapping him on the back, Jared could sense the two of them felt the same satisfaction in how life had turned out. There were so many twists and turns along the way, so many ways that things could have been different, that Jared might never have met Sugar or experienced this level of gratification with Asal doting on Violet and his mother doting on Sugar.

For the moment, Jared swallowed away the tightness in his throat, and the memory of his sixteenth birthday surfaced. The range targets had been reset, and as sixteenth birthdays went, that one had kicked ass. Dad let him have full pick of all of his weapons. It was a dad-son day of ammo and target practice. Jared had played down how pumped he was, but between that and his mom offering to make his favorite dinner, that day couldn't have been any better.

He loved the heavy weight of the .45 in his hand, the cold feel of the metal, and how it warmed to his touch. He'd caressed the side with his fingertip, and the target had been his. Jared hadn't yet stepped to the line, and he knew that bull's-eye would be hollowed out with his shots.

Dad had cleared his throat. "You given any thought to college?"

That was the one topic they didn't talk much about. School had sent home letter after letter reminding his parents how he was a candidate for great things. He had grades and the leadership skills—qualities that colleges apparently recruited.

"No." He'd stepped to the line, and the world disappeared. When his target was in sight, Jared had tunnel vision. There was an instinctual focus that he couldn't describe. It was predatory—or perhaps evolutionary, further drilled into him by his father. There was no option other than completing his objective. A direct hit, no matter what distractions the world offered. *Like college applications.*

He emptied his clip, leaving a hollowed-out target, and turned to look at his dad's approving profile. "I'm going to be a Ranger."

Much like now, he knew with certainty that he was

going to continue to excel in his job as family man.

Most people who said they wanted to be Army Rangers didn't have a shot in hell. But even at sixteen, he wasn't most people.

At the time, his Dad's jaw flexed, his eyes crinkling at the corners as he took in the obliterated target. A minute passed by, and an unspoken conversation occurred between them. It wasn't one of convincing or persuasion. It was not a mental mano a mano but a simple realization between two men cut from the same cloth.

Dad had nodded. "I'll make sure to tell your mother." Now, standing in the hospital room with his own family, he was sure that whatever his children came to him with, Jared would have that same conviction in them that his father had in his dreams.

"You're an excellent father," Dad said. "When you decide to do something well, you do just that."

The way his father said things, his man-of-few-words, always-speak-the-truth approach to life, it meant a lot. "I had good role models."

"Your mother more so than me." Dad laughed.

Mom joined in with his laughter. "I'd agree with that."

Jared remembered the day during Sugar's pregnancy when she had dropped the baby-name book to the top of her protruding stomach. "We should call her Violet."

"What—like my mom?"

"Exactly like your mom."

"Why?" Jared asked.

"You surround yourself with strong women. She was the first."

"True…" Violet Westin. There was already one of those, and she was a live wire. "But…"

"The woman practically tore down a burning building to save her son." Sugar's eyes had gone watery. "I want that name attached to our daughter."

Damn. One of the scariest days of his life—he was man enough to admit that now—had been when his mom almost died because she loved him that much.

After his dad had gone back in to the burning house, his parents apparently walked out of it holding hands—holding each other up—but through the smoke and the fire, his mother had methodically searched for her son. *A mother's love.*

As Jared had grown up, he'd watched her deal with his antics and rule with an iron fist—and love with a giant heart. She kept the troops—what she called their family, including anyone needing a shoulder to lean on—in line.

So accepting Sugar's choice of names hadn't been difficult. She'd tried the name out, slowly saying, "Violet Westin."

"Violet *Lilly* Westin," Jared had said. "For the two strongest women I know."

Sugar's decision reached her eyes, and the name had been agreed to before Sugar could even mouth the word "yes" and kiss him.

He took a deep breath, focusing back on the maternity room in front of him.

The baby stirred, and Sugar's dark-blue eyes drifted open. "I'm going to give this nursing thing a try again."

Asal, Jenny, and Jared's mom helped her sit up and futz with pillows as Asher and Jared opened up the food bags. Dad took a food order from his wife and Jenny and Asher and went to grab more cafeteria grub. Asal, apparently done directing her mom on the idiosyncrasies of nursing a newborn, hopped down and grabbed her lunch, pulling a chair to the table and tucking her knees under her as she got comfortable.

"God, I'm talented." Sugar squealed, and Jared looked over. She nursed the baby while drinking out of a large hospital mug. "Small victories. Don't knock 'em."

He tossed a fry into his mouth. "I can't imagine the complexities happening over there. You just flag for a refill."

She beamed, and when Violet let loose for a minute, Sugar gave her drink to Jenny, grumbling. "If anyone says this is a piece of cake at first, they can bite my booty."

Jenny and his mother agreed, and a few minutes later they heard one serious baby belch that could rival few of the guys on his team. His mom held his newborn, and Jenny snapped pictures. All was right in their world.

"So what else is happening?" Dad asked.

"I've hired a few new guys."

"For the main team?"

Jared nodded. "And I'm expanding Delta. Brock's taking the lead on that."

"Good." Dad turned to Asher. "How about you? Everything still stinks in Washington. Having fun with that? Or about done?"

"Jenny's about to announce she's headlining something on Broadway," Asher replied.

"Ah, the politician deflects." Dad elbowed Asher good-naturedly.

"I didn't know that!" Sugar said. "Why didn't I know?"

"You had things going on. *Like a baby.*"

"Oh, BS. Asher's throwing you under the bus. What aren't you telling us?" Sugar's eyebrows went up. "You *are* going to announce your candidacy soon, aren't you?"

He laughed and shook his head, a dead McIntyre giveaway. "Come on, Sugar. We're here for you."

"Yay! This is so exciting."

Again, Asher shook his head, this time not doing a great job of hiding his pearly-white smile. "Nothing is official."

"It never is," Sugar squeaked. "Holy moley. My sister will be First Lady of the United States. Do you know how crazy that is to say out loud?"

"*Could be.*" Jenny bit her bottom lip. "We'll see. Things happen."

Sugar decided to torture her sister later with that. "But you're headlining Broadway? That's crazy cool."

"Way cooler. And a certainty." Asher threw his arm around Jenny. "She's amazing."

Jared backed up and stared at his family. This room was full of impossible dreamers, surpassing what once could have only been a hope and a wish.

A Broadway headliner and a presidential candidate? His wife and children? Behind his family and friends was a group of warriors that he'd brought together for a greater good. Damn. Life was pretty fuckin' great.

Asal fidgeted in the corner now that her lunch was done and the baby and all of the room's guests were old news.

Jenny took her hand. "Want to go explore?"

"Yes!"

Asher grabbed a couple things for Asal. "We actually told Mia we'd take Asal out for the afternoon."

Jared shook his hand. "Thanks." Then he gave his little girl a kiss and sent her packing. His mom had the baby, who had nestled back asleep in a corner in a chair. His dad grabbed another chair.

140

"What do you think, Boss Man? Think we can break out of here soon?" Sugar asked.

"You're raring to go that fast?"

Her blue eyes danced. "I want to get back to our life."

His heart swelled. "Soon as we get a stamp of approval, we'll be on our way. I'm good with that."

"Take as much help from the hospital and nurses as you can while you're here." His mom stood, kissed the baby, and gave her to him. "And rest while you can. We'll come over and help."

"Thanks."

Jared repositioned Violet so that he could stare down and watch her sleep. She fit inside his forearm even with the blanket wrapped around her. She was no longer than a football and weighed less than a brick of ammo. Vi-vi was...vulnerable. Precious. She was dependent on Sugar for nutrition, but damn if he wouldn't provide for everything else.

She opened her little mouth and yawned. Even at full stretch, everything about her was tiny. She had a smattering of dark hair, and when she did open her eyes, they were blue. Jared leaned his head closer. "Hey, Vi."

More than one person had said newborns didn't smile after he announced that his daughter smiled at him. But he swore to God that Violet just smiled again.

"Oh, one more thing." His mom reached into her

bag and pulled out a pink-wrapped box. "One more thing. I couldn't resist."

The *you didn't have to*s were said, and Sugar opened the box. It was a pink-camo onesie with, in military block print, "Titan Princess in Training."

"Wow, Mom." He picked up the outfit, running his thumb over the words.

She gave him a knowing look. "Sooner or later, you'll have to be ready for the next generation of Titan."

He thought about his teams, the new recruits, the men who'd been with him since day one, the paternity-leave requests, the women who had joined their ranks, and the babies and kids who ran the halls of Titan HQ. "We already are."

ABOUT THE AUTHOR

Cristin Harber is a New York Times and USA Today bestselling romance author. She writes romantic suspense, military romance, new adult, and contemporary romance. Readers voted her onto Amazon's Top Picks for Debut Romance Authors in 2013, and her debut Titan series was both a #1 romantic suspense and #1 military romance bestseller.

Join the newsletter! Text TITAN to 66866 to sign up for exclusive emails.

Made in United States
Troutdale, OR
05/08/2024

19724005R00094